His gaze swept over her from top to bottom, embarrassing her with its blatant scrutiny. He extended his arm and shook her offered hand. She observed the warmth, the roughness, the largeness of it, and a mysterious heat seeped through her. She noted with dismay the blush stealing up her neck as she waited for him to acknowledge their connection.

"A pleasure." Her boldness obviously amused him. Sitting back casually in his chair, he draped one arm over the back of it as he regarded her. "You know, with the sun shining through that window, it looked like your entire head had caught fire. Remarkable."

He'd been staring at her hair? Surely, he teased, but nothing in his expression indicated humor. He didn't know her identity, that much was clear. When she merely stood there with a questioning frown, he raised an eyebrow. She felt like a fool as he sat there staring at her, his arrogance prickling, like a burr under her saddle blanket.

Then suddenly he smiled at her, and it struck her dumb, before she realized that due to her lack of anything to say, she was the source of his amusement.

Praise for Deb Ransburg

A Witch to Burn For, by Deb Ransburg

Aristocrat Avery shows kindness to the poor villager Fiona when her grandmother is burned as a witch. That good deed, and his attraction to her, begin a series of events that places them both in grave danger. It takes magic, and love, to put things right again.

"Ransburg's strong characters, vivid setting, and clever plot make this an engaging, quick read. Highly recommended for those who enjoy paranormal and historical romance."

~ *Lynn Lovegreen, YA historical romance author*

Minding Millie

by

Deb Ransburg

Minding Millie

Cover Art by *The Wild Rose Press, Inc.*

The Wild Rose Press, Inc.
PO Box 708
Adams Basin, NY 14410-0708
Visit us at www.thewildrosepress.com

Publishing History
First Edition, 2023
Trade Paperback ISBN 978-1-5092-5023-3
Digital ISBN 978-1-5092-5024-0

Published in the United States of America

Chapter One

Kansas-1884

Margaret Carroll neatly folded the note in her hand and tucked it carefully back into the envelope in which it had arrived. It was obvious who'd crafted this threat. In order to avoid displaying his handwriting, the sender had cut words from the newspaper, pasting them into a message which left little to the imagination. The missive in her hand, by itself, didn't seem all that threatening, but the purpose and intent packed the sufficient punch to leave her shaking with anger.

The threat was about her fortune, obviously, which was nothing new. But until now, no one had ever threatened her life for it.

As far as she was concerned, the fortune meant little to her. But she'd be damned if she'd give it up. All she had, all she'd accumulated over her sixty-some years on this earth, had never really belonged to her. She'd guarded her wealth so vigilantly because of only one person.

Her granddaughter.

Millie had earned every penny she stood to inherit, not because of the blood running through her veins, but because of the person she'd become. A loving granddaughter, Millie took care of Margaret without complaint, no easy task. She was a sincere girl, who'd never asked for anything without working relentlessly to earn it. Margaret took great pride in her granddaughter, and the only way to repay her, for her love and care and so much more, was to offer her a life of freedom when Margaret herself left this world.

She never wanted Millie to be forced to compromise herself, simply because she'd be alone when Margaret died. Margaret understood the plight of a woman alone in this world. Even a blind man on a runaway horse could see how events would play out. Scoundrels would come at Millie like pigs to the trough once she died. Hungry, flashy, grinning rats would come from near and far for one crack at her fabled holdings.

And if by some miracle, there happened to be one man with pure intentions, he would be hard to sift from the other rubbish storming her door. Margaret never wanted Millie to act out of desperation, feeling she had no choice but to rely on some slippery, self-serving tyrant for her survival. So, yes, Margaret had guarded her fortune faithfully to protect her granddaughter from the wolves who would, no doubt, prey upon Millie upon Margaret's death.

Now, here in this late hour of her life, some villain intended to take it from her upon threat of murder. Well, she wouldn't have it.

Her fortune was not the only backstop she'd crafted. Wheels were in motion. Indeed, they were. No one could outmaneuver Margaret Carroll when it came to the welfare of the one person who deserved the security and peace she could offer through the fortune she'd accumulated.

This threat, apparently meant to intimidate her, scare her, bully her into giving up what she'd worked a lifetime to secure for her granddaughter, wouldn't work.

Child's play.

Margaret Carroll had been preparing for this moment her entire life, knowing sooner or later all of her wealth and good fortune would bring an ugly darkness to her door. She was relieved it had finally shown itself, this shadow which had followed her since her husband's death, and she would take it on eagerly, loving a good challenge more than anything. No one played the game better than she did.

****

"You're awfully quiet, Millie."

Millie and Grammie sat together on their front porch, a time which usually provided easy conversation.

"Sorry, Grammie." Millie glanced sideways at the old woman. "I guess I'm not good company today."

"And you were daydreaming throughout the sermon."

Margaret professed to be a devout Christian every Sunday. The rest of the week, however, she was inclined to cuss, chew, and embarrass those of more delicate sensibilities with her bold, ribald humor. Millie gave her a raised eyebrow, calling her out on her temporary piety.

None of the other parishioners in their small community would dare call her out, however. Common sense dictated staying on Grammie's good side, not only because of her tendency to browbeat, but also because she could easily claim to be the richest person in the five-county area.

Her grandmother, small in stature, stood larger than life to Millie, and Millie loved her sorely. She broached the subject which had plagued her through church service. "I've been thinking about Parker. Do you think

I was wrong to reject him?"

"Humph!" Grammie would say little on the matter. She did, however, manage an impressive stream of spit from the tobacco concealed in her cheek.

Millie hid her smile. "You don't like Parker much, do you?"

Grammie looked at her sideways. "I'm glad you had enough sense to turn down his proposal."

"You know I value your opinion. What was it about him you disliked?" she asked, hoping for some insight. She'd yet to pinpoint exactly what had caused her own dislike.

"You have to ask?" A pronounced frown marked Grammie's features.

Millie twisted her auburn curls and lifted the thick mass off her neck to dry the moisture forming there. She took a deep breath and sighed in resignation. Releasing her hair as the scorching heat of the day settled in on the plains, she unbuttoned the stiff collar of her Sunday dress.

"Let me guess," Millie huffed. "Just another money grubber, drawn here from who knows where?"

Margaret stared ahead, indicating she had no argument with the assessment.

That a fortune hunter would go to the trouble of courting her and propose marriage, because of the reputation of a man she'd never even met, still astounded her. "How well known was my grandfather?" Millie asked with humor.

Grammie's face softened. "Let's just say his notoriety stretched quite a-ways, and not only for his wealth. He was a powerful man. Handsome too. But he only had eyes for me." She grinned with pride.

"You're lucky to have had him, Gram. When men look at me, all they see is a dollar sign." Sometimes discouragement seeped to the bone; this latest fiasco with Parker only fueling her frustration.

"Millie! That's simply not true," her grandmother insisted. "You're a beautiful girl."

Millie shrugged. "It doesn't matter what I look like," she told her. "A man will never simply see me, without a worth appraisal. Sometimes I wish people didn't know so much about us. Maybe then someone would see me and not your money."

Grammie harrumphed. "The men around here aren't worth a damn. There are people, maybe not here, but there are those who will see you for you."

Millie appreciated the words of encouragement from her grandmother, but she wouldn't likely meet any of those people. LaBelle didn't exactly draw a lot of travelers.

They stood to go inside, the heat of the day bearing down on them in their Sunday finery. The kitchen sat at the back of the large farmhouse and meant the sun didn't penetrate the shades of daylight in the room. The pale, spring-green paint of the kitchen walls offered a cool reprieve to the eyes. The brown floor tiles were cool and clean. A slight breeze stirred the curtains, but all of this did little to cool the humid, August air. And though lunch smelled delicious, the heat diminished Millie's appetite considerably. She tore at the chafing collar of her dress, preferring the comfort of pants and the loose-fitting shirts. Putting water on for tea, she plopped her drooping form heavily on a chair, when Grammie's words jolted her right back out of it.

"I should tell you, I sent your father a letter a few

months back. Don't know if it reached him or not."

Millie's heart pounded in her chest. Grammie had never willingly mentioned her father, and she'd stopped asking questions about him years ago. "My father? Why on earth would you do that? You haven't spoken to him since he left."

Grammie's waved her hand in dismissal. "I knew he'd be wondering about you, so I wrote him and told him what he expected to hear. Not much truth, not lies exactly."

Millie had long wished for some connection to her father, some news, information, or story about him. But her stubborn grandmother had shut the topic down many years ago. It must be something important for her to break years of stonewalling.

"What did you tell him?" she asked, trying to sound casual.

Grammie's response erupted as something between a snort and a giggle. She took a deep breath and exhaled loudly. "I told him what he wanted to hear, that I'd ruined you by spoiling you rotten."

A sensation she couldn't identify washed through Millie. "Is that all?"

"Well, I told him I was dying, which isn't necessarily a lie. I mean everybody's dying, if you think on it." Grammie turned and pretended to look for something in the pantry. "I enjoyed writing that letter. I truly did. I can't wait for him to meet you. He won't know what to think."

"Meet me?" Millie practically squeaked. "It's not likely we'll ever meet." She grabbed a roll from the basket in front of her. Realizing she had no appetite, she tossed it back.

"Why?" Millie asked. And she meant "why" to all of it. Why now? Why trickery? Why had the man who'd disappeared before even a memory had formed of him, been wrenched back into their lives after nineteen years? And how could Grammie be so blasted cavalier about it all?

"I want him to come for you." She smiled a queer smile, hiding some perverted secret. "It's time for you to know him."

Frustration burned in Millie's chest. She felt close to tears, but she didn't cry. She wouldn't start now. "Why did you describe me like, well, like Bridget?" Grammie comparing her to her rude and obnoxious cousin appalled Millie.

Grammie's eyes bored into hers. "To confuse him," she admitted, as if it were perfectly obvious. "He'll expect you to be like her, and he'll be so befuddled when he meets you, it'll wipe away all his prejudice. He'll have to begin from scratch in getting to know you, just like you said earlier. Your pa will have spent years imagining all the ways I've ruined you. I know him, and he's spent these years convincing himself I've spoiled you rotten, and he's better off not knowing you. If he thinks I'm dying, he'll have to come for you, see? He'll know you have nowhere else to go. He won't shirk his duty by you. I know that."

"Grammie, I've dreaded the day, but it has finally come. You've gone absolutely daft."

Grammie wagged her finger at Millie, "You need a change, a fresh perspective, to meet new people. You stated as much yourself."

Millie sighed in resignation, suddenly overwhelmingly tired. She'd be the first to admit she grew restless. But she belonged with her grandmother, and she couldn't conceive of another life, didn't want to imagine beginning a different one.

"Well, I don't see what my father has to do with either of us." She observed her grandmother with a narrowed gaze, but Gram seemed intent on avoiding culpability by not looking directly at her. "Listen, Grammie. My father has never so much as contacted me. You're wrong to assume he'll swoop in and suddenly want to know me. You and this ranch are my life. I like it that way, and I'll never leave. So, before you go stirring up a hornet's nest, you should take my feelings into consideration." She stood and kissed the old woman on the cheek, dismissing the topic. Her mind churned, buried emotions bubbling up "Is it okay if I skip lunch? I want to go for a ride."

Grammie waved her away. "You go on. It's too damned hot to eat, anyway."

The old woman watched Millie leave and smiled to herself.

"Your feelings, Millie, darlin', are first and foremost on my mind."

Chapter Two

Wyoming

The steady pounding of rain outside helped ease the beating of his brains against his skull only a little. Raine McConnell leisurely opened his eyes, his arms wrapped tightly around a crumpled pillow, his long legs still in his jeans, tangled in a mess of blankets, and his head throbbing like drums in a marching band. The open window of the cabin allowed the cold air to fill the small room and ease the nausea in his stomach.

When he'd set his mind to getting drunk last night, he'd known he'd wake up with a hell of a hangover, but he hadn't counted on one with this intensity. He stood, testing first the strength of his long legs, and then the sturdiness of his stomach, which he found questionable. Hopefully, Tom would be in the main house with coffee.

Outside, he stretched his cramped muscles and pulled fresh air deep into his lungs to ease his dizziness. Putting his fist inside of his hat, he removed the dent in the crown, set the crumpled remains on his head, and trotted down the path to the main house. Pausing outside on the front porch long enough to make out Tom's voice, and then Jake Lansford's, his cohort in debauchery the night before, he opened the door and walked to the dining room. The amused looks confronting him when he pulled out his chair across from the two men prompted a slight wave of self-reproach.

He sat down and pulled himself up to the table, resting his face in his hands, hoping to ease the pounding headache. "Did I miss breakfast?"

"Yup," Jake answered.

"Damn," Raine muttered. "Is anything left? I need something in my stomach."

At that moment, the cook brought in a plate of steaming eggs, potatoes, and sausages. The smell made his mouth water. He looked up at her with a sheepish grin. "You're a saint, Ruth."

"And you couldn't be further from one." She gave him her most disapproving frown but winked at Tom as she turned away.

Tom stood up and started pacing, eager for Raine to finish his breakfast. Scratching two days' worth of stubble on his cheek, he sighed. "I need te talk to ye when you're done."

Jake hid a smile behind his fist and cleared his throat, trying not to chuckle. "Aw, Tom. You ain't gonna yell at him, are ya?"

Tom turned. Raine scowled at Jake.

"Of course not." He observed Raine, seriousness marking his brow. "He's a grown man. Though I'd imagine he was up to enough trouble last night to deserve a reprimand."

"Nonsense," Raine told him. "I've been in the line cabin since November." He sat back, rubbing his temples. "Is it a crime for a man to drink his share of whiskey?"

Tom cleared his throat, trying not to chuckle. "Your share and how many others'?"

"Well, I'm gonna head out. I'm sure you have plenty

to discuss. See you boys." Jake stood, for all appearances a man eager to make his exit. "There's fence to mend, when you can get to it. Some stock escaped last night. Don't you worry that pretty head of yours none, though, Raine. I rounded 'em all back up early this mornin'."

"I'll walk you out." Tom followed Jake onto the front porch. Jake mounted his horse, and Tom gave him a slight nod and a smile as he rode off.

Raine shoveled the remainder of crispy potatoes into his mouth and pushed himself away from the table, still chewing. Retrieving a clean shirt from the laundry room, he pushed his arms through the sleeves and buttoned it as he joined Tom on the porch.

"Shall we ride?" Tom asked.

At Raine's nod, they headed for the corral, their boots clomping heavily on the split rail steps. Their horses were saddled and waiting. Tom checked his saddle, tugging on the cinch to tighten it.

"What got into you last night?"

"Nothing besides a little too much whiskey," Raine answered with a wince. "Guess I felt bulletproof."

"Know what I think? I think ye've been putting everything you have into this ranch for so long, you've forgotten a man's supposed to build a life somewhere along the way. I think every once in a while you remember that, and you drink yourself into a stupor, tryin' to forget."

"I think you have too much time on your hands, if you have time to sit around and rationalize why I got drunk—for the first time in months, I might add."

As they moved into the sunlight, Tom could see Raine's green pallor and dazed expression. "Are ye okay?"

Raine adjusted his hat over short black hair, which curled a touch at his temples and neck. "Yeah. I just need a ride and a bit of fresh air."

They mounted their horses and turned east into the sun. Tom shook his head and laughed. "I don't think you're going to get off that easily."

Raine winced with a laugh. "You're probably right. What did you want to talk about?"

Tom looked at the reins in his hands and purposefully studied a crack in the leather. "Did I ever tell you I had a daughter?"

Raine searched his memory through the fog still lingering there. "Kansas, wasn't it?"

"Yeah," Tom answered. His mouth clenched in a somber frown for some time. His voice cracked when he spoke. "When my wife died, her mother took my daughter from me." He looked up at Raine. "Finding you was the only thing that saved me back then." He shifted uncomfortably. "I hoped I could offer you a good life, and I was looking to fill the hole in my heart."

Raine nodded silently, waiting for Tom to organize his thoughts and tell him what weighed so heavily on his mind.

Thomas grunted. "You were such an angry young thing. That was understandable after what they did to your people at Sand Creek. You'd seen some horrors. I wanted to earn your trust, convince you I'd not be making a slave out of ye, nor a whipping post."

Indeed, it hadn't been easy for Tom to earn his trust after purchasing him in that saloon. Raine remembered those first few days with Tom: the endless prairie, the tedious squeak of wagon wheels, days of staring at the passing ground through the hole at his feet, trail dust burning his eyes and lungs, relentless heat, and the absolute despair he'd experienced at the loss of his family.

"You saved me, Tom. I couldn't have asked for a better life than the one you've given me."

Tom grunted again and squinted into the sun as he looked out ahead of them. "And you saved me."

"What about your daughter?"

He spoke, a brittle edge to his voice. "I've heard from her grandmother. Good ol' Margaret. It took a while for her letter to get here." He studied the reins again. "I wish it hadno'," he added softly.

"Want to tell me what you're hem-hawing around about?" Raine asked, sensing his hesitancy.

They faced each other. "I need you to go to Kansas and bring her back to live with us." Tom chuckled when Raine winced. "I'd like to tell you it won't be bad, but from what Margaret says…" Squinting, he paused to recollect the exact description. "She wrote that my daughter is 'beautiful, not sensible, but always a lady'. I read that part several times."

Raine grimaced, despite the sympathy he felt for Tom. To have his daughter taken from him as an infant and to never know her was one thing. But to have her thrown back in his life twenty years later had to bring all the pain into focus. The girl had become a stranger to him.

"Do you really want to take on something like that?" he asked.

"If it weren't for the fact that her grandmother is ancient, I'd say 'no'. I've been this long without her in my life. But Margaret seems to think she needs looking after. Frankly, I don't see why the old woman doesn't just marry her off."

When Raine offered no counter, Tom said, "I wish it could be otherwise, Son. But she is my daughter."

"Don't apologize to me." Raine balked that Tom needed to defend himself. They'd been through too much together and understood each other too well. "I just hope she's not as bad as you're imagining, for your sake."

"I had hopes that things would turn out differently."

"How so?"

"For years, when you were younger, I harbored a secret wish that the girl would come to me, and the two of you…"

Raine laughed, his blue eyes lighting with amusement. "Are you trying to marry me off?"

"No. No, son. It's just that…" He stopped, shaking his graying head in disbelief. "I'm sounding like an old woman. As simple witted as it is, I used to hope she'd be someone special, someone good enough for you, someone that could make you happy. I'd hate to see you end up a lonely old man like me. You need a woman in your life… a family."

"I'm doing just fine alone."

"Oh, really? Are you going to make nights like last night a regular occurrence? Are you going to keep yourself holed up at the line cabin until you become a crazy old man? Face it, Raine. You're lonely. A wife and family can be very fulfilling."

"And that worked out well for you, did it? One night I drink too much, suddenly I'm a lost soul." Raine hoped he could snuff Tom's fantasies. "Why would you want to marry me to your daughter, anyway? I have nothing except what I've saved working for you. You know it's more than enough for me, but it would never be enough for someone like the girl you describe."

"Working for me?" Hurt crossed Tom's features, as well as anger, at the reservations Raine had about their relationship. "Everything will be yours, Raine. I've known you since you were a wee chip who took on a regiment of soldiers, intent on hurting you, and I've loved ye like my own since the day I found ye. You're my son, as much as my own flesh and blood."

Raine protested, but Tom raised his hand. "Ye know how I feel abote ye, lad." The heavy brogue, which had lessened over the years, slipped back into his speech. "I wouldno' want anyone else tae have it." He shook his head, clearly frustrated that he'd become emotional. "Besides the fact that she has a considerable fortune coming to her when her grandmother dies, you've worked this ranch harder than I have. If it hadn't been for you, I wouldn't have survived the hard times. It belongs to you." Stubborn lines creased his rugged face.

"It should be your daughter's." Raine returned the hard look. He already owed Tom a debt he could never repay.

"Damn it, man. I don't even know the lass's name. Besides, what would she do with the ranch, but let it go to ruin?"

"You don't know that for certain."

"Yes, I do. She's just like her mother. Spoiled."

Raine raised an inquisitive brow.

"I fell for her mother hard. I believed I loved her, but looking back, 'overwhelmed' might be a better description. She charmed the pants off me. But I realized soon after our marriage that she needed a lot of tending. I believe she cared for me, and that made it all worthwhile." Tom scratched his head, a nervous habit.

Raine regarded the older man, and Tom continued, "It's hard to believe they both turned out so fragile. When you meet Margaret, it will surprise you, too. She's one tough old vulture. I used to like her, really respect her, before she took the baby. I know she had her own reasons. She grieved for Amanda and probably blamed me. Still, I canna forgive her."

They rode in silence until they came upon another gap in the border fence of their Lazy Ace land. Raine glanced to the right where several of their cattle grazed with leisure on the other side. He couldn't help but think about the losses they'd both faced.

"You've been pretty happy over the years, despite everything, haven't you, Tom?"

"I have." Tom had never allowed himself to think what his life would have been like had he had his daughter to raise and love, because he might never have met Raine. And he couldn't imagine loving his daughter more than he did his adopted son. Thinking of things that couldn't be was pointless. He liked to deal with the facts of his life. But if the truth be told, there were times he wondered.

"Come on, son. Let's mend this fence."

Chapter Three

Millie and her best friend, Lydia, enjoyed an invigorating ride down by the river, as they did every Sunday afternoon. As summer neared its end, the riversides were lush with green grass and proud, full trees. On any other Sunday, Millie would be content to laze her afternoon away on those wealthy banks, but today an eagerness to get home fueled her.

"You won again, Mill. You always win." Lydia, breathless with the exertion of their ride, rode up behind Millie and dismounted her sorrel gelding.

"No, I don't, Lyddie. Why, just last week…"

"You let me win." Lydia finished for her.

"How could you say such a thing?"

"You think I'm so stupid that I believe this old puddin' foot could beat Outlaw? Don't insult me." Millie rummaged for an explanation, and Lydia smiled at her. "But I do appreciate it. My ego needs the nourishment, even if it is all gum."

"As if your ego needs any fueling," Millie answered.

Lydia laughed, dismounted, and perched herself upon the railing of the stall. Their weekly ritual unfolded as Millie took pleasure in caring for the horses, and Lydia relayed the latest gossip from town. Pulling the saddle off her horse, Millie began pitching out clean hay for both resting horses, but her mind drifted elsewhere as

Lydia began chatting.

She'd already anxiously relayed the news to Lydia of the letter from her father. She'd never shared the story of her parents, even with Lydia, until today. She'd pushed the hurt of losing both her parents deep inside, only to have that pain pulled forth again suddenly. Her mind raced with speculation as she listened halfheartedly to Lydia's latest gossip, an episode involving Mrs. Fredrickson, the minister, and the Communion wine. She pitched hay with unusual vigor, and she didn't notice when Lydia stopped talking. Silence came just as naturally between them as conversation, but she soon realized her mistake of ignoring what to Lydia constituted a monumental story. Slapping her horse on the rear and sending him off to eat, she straightened and gave her friend an apologetic glance.

Lydia descended from her perch and hooked her arm through Millie's.

"What kind of man do you imagine your father is?" she asked as they walked arm in arm.

They were an unusual pair, contrasting each other starkly. Lydia was short and voluptuous, her brown, straight hair pulled back neatly with pins, hardly one out of place. Millie was tall in contrast, long-limbed and lean from years of physical work. Her dark auburn hair, even when pulled back and braided with a thin band of leather, still formed a mass of unruly curls, none of which pointed in any particular direction, giving her the appearance of just having weathered a windstorm. She envied Lydia's neat, well-presented appearance, as she'd never perfected the details of grooming, which seemed to come so easily to her friend.

They walked in stride together toward the house, a

refreshing glass of tea their goal, when Millie suddenly halted, pushing Lydia behind the barn and out of sight.

"Holy Moses," she whispered, mostly to herself. She peeked back around the corner and watched as a man she'd never seen dismounted his horse in front of the house.

Lydia patiently stood behind her, until her curiosity overcame her, and she too peeked around the barn. As the stranger entered Grammie's house, Lydia just missed seeing him. When Lydia looked up at Millie, her face screwed up in question.

"What's the matter?" Lydia whispered.

Millie's brows drew together, and then she shrugged. Chewing on a thumbnail, she started back for the house, with Lydia close behind her. Suddenly, she pulled up short and turned to Lydia, who almost ran right into her.

Her mind was a jumble of fragmented imaginings. Her brows drew together again as she looked to the house. Why had Grammie written to her father after all this time? Who was that stranger, she wondered? What scheme had Grammie concocted? "You know," She dismissed the stranger she'd just seen and focused on the topic at hand. "My father could be a drunkard who would've beaten me senseless, or some kind of criminal, for heaven's sake. I don't know why I bother giving him a second thought."

"What were you looking at, Millie?" Lydia asked.

"What?" She didn't really mean to be evasive.

Lydia arched one brow. "You know, trying to carry on a conversation with you is like trying to pull a single string out of a very thick rope."

"Sorry." Knowing if she could barely keep track of

her own thinking, it would completely thwart Lydia in the attempt.

Lydia smiled as she looped her arm through Millie's again. "No need. Come on. Feed me. I'm famished."

They entered the house, and Millie looked around casually for the man she'd seen outside. The door to the parlor remained closed, which would indicate Grammie had secluded herself in there with him.

Who was he? Why was he here? It was just so odd. This quiet community lay well off the beaten path. Strangers rarely passed through, much less stopped in these parts. Curiosity erupted when Parker had come, with no family hereabout, and announced his intention to set up his law practice. Now a tall, dark, handsome man had appeared in her very home, and Millie's overactive imagination couldn't contain itself. Who was he? Where did he come from? Why was he here? She couldn't very well put her ear to the door and eavesdrop—well, at least not with Lyddie standing there, her stomach rumbling loudly enough to alert Grammie and the stranger of their presence.

"Okay, okay." She laughed at Lydia, who stood impatiently with her arms crossed and a slight scowl on her face. "To the kitchen!" She pointed in the direction. "Grammie fried chicken after church, and there's corn, green beans, and rolls. Will that be enough?"

At her friend's nod, she led Lydia to the kitchen, where they found her cousin, Bridget, seated at the table, having just finished her lunch and wiping her mouth primly on a napkin.

"Hey, Bridge," she offered.

Bridget rolled her eyes at Millie and belched into her napkin. Millie pulled out a chair and took a seat across from Bridget, pouring Lydia and herself a glass of tea. Lydia sat down between the cousins. Accustomed to Bridget, she was able to overlook her cousin's unusual greeting. Lydia ignored her, however, unable to abide Bridget's usual rudeness.

"What's going on around here? Do you know?" Millie asked.

Bridget narrowed her eyes, and Millie braced herself for the inevitable verbal attack. Bridget's expression indicated something had upset her. It could have been anything from an ingrown toenail to her bodice being too tight, but as usual, she intended to take her aggravation out on Millie.

"Grammie's still going on about your long-lost father up there in the wilds of Wyoming." She tugged at her bodice and cleared her throat. "When are ya'll gonna get it in your heads, that if that man gave a hoot about you, you'd be with him instead of with Grammie? Face it. As soon as your momma died, he skedaddled. He wanted nothing to do with you." With that, she stood, brushed the crumbs from the front of her dress onto the floor, dropped her napkin onto her plate, and walked out.

The friends sat in silence, chewing on Bridget's words, until Lydia finally sighed.

"Don't tell me you're going to let her bother you? What does she know?"

Millie shook off the effects of Bridget's taunts and sighed, too.

"She's right though. That's the only thing that really galls me, is that for once she's right, and she'll never stop gloating."

Millie smiled at her friend, took a sip of her tea, drumming her fingers absently on the tabletop. Her mind turned over furiously enough to be heard. She looked through the kitchen doorway toward the parlor and pursed her lips as she remembered the man she'd seen, knowing he remained in there with Grammie, but not knowing why.

Lydia sighed loudly, showing her exasperation with Millie. "Do you want to tell me what else is bothering you, or do I have to sit here and starve until I guess at what has your face all twisted in a pinch?"

"There was a man." She hesitated, reluctant to divulge. "I saw him come in, so he's in there with Grammie right now."

"Well, that is curious." Lydia straightened in her chair. "It wasn't someone you know, I assume?"

Millie shook her head and then bit her lower lip.

"What about him then?" Lydia leaned forward in her chair at Millie's flushed cheeks.

"I swear, Lyddie," Millie said, her voice low and breathless. "He had to be the most sinfully handsome man I've ever seen."

****

Behind the closed doors of Margaret Carroll's parlor, Raine stood before the old woman with a grim expression, his hands folded, holding his hat in front of him. As haughty as any queen giving audience to the disdained, she sat in stoic silence, scrutinizing him with probing eyes. Those eyes, a much less vibrant green than they must have been in her youth, appeared ready to pop out of their sockets, made worse by the spectacles perched on her pronounced nose. It was exceedingly disconcerting to get a glare from such a pair of eyes.

"What kind of name is 'Raine'?" she barked, breaking the silence between them.

An immediate dislike for the old woman washed through him. Tom was right. She was cantankerous. And what she'd done to Tom didn't help his opinion of her. His patience, already worn thin from weeks of hard travel, threatened to snap at her boorishness. She'd not even offered him a seat. Even with his backwoods upbringing, he understood the rudeness of it.

"A given one."

"Damn foolish name," she muttered, examining his form from head to boot tip.

Raine glowered, holding his retort in check.

"Are you married, son?"

He weighed the significance of her interest in his marital status. He didn't like the direction his suspicions led him. She was old. Ancient.

"No." He shook himself mentally. "The reason I'm here…" He began.

Margaret held up her hand and waved him into silence. "I know why you're here." At his raised eyebrow, she finished, "Thomas sent you?"

Thomas had predicted Raine would arrive well before his last letter, and then he'd muttered something about the 'element of surprise'. So, how had she known he was coming?

"Yes." He shifted his hat in his hands. "You received his letter…?"

"No," she interrupted again. "But I'm good at deductions. Not many strangers pass through these parts."

He wiped his brow. He had no doubt of that. A sane person would sooner vacation in hell than to travel here purposely. He couldn't believe the heat this late in the year.

Margaret Carroll stood with little effort, considering her advanced years. He watched her walk to the sideboard and pour herself a whiskey. She offered him a drink by holding the bottle in the air and waggling it a bit. He refused with a slight shake of his head.

"I…" he tried again in vain.

"You're a right handsome fella. Can't understand why you wouldn't be married. Are you afflicted in some way?"

He ignored her misplaced curiosity, and her third interruption in less than two minutes, to state his business. "Thomas McConnell?"

"What has Thomas made of himself over these years?" Her unwavering stare, coupled with her bluntness, unnerved him. It put him on the defensive and he didn't like it. He prided himself on being in control of any situation.

Grinding his teeth, he endeavored to keep his tongue civil. "He sent me here to escort his daughter back to Wyoming."

"He's had a satisfying life? Gone out and made something of himself?"

He frowned. Why did this old woman give a damn about Tom's happiness? He supposed she retained a misplaced sense of guilt, and he would not give her the satisfaction of an answer.

Margaret Carroll, however, would not let it go so easily, and fully under her unnerving glare, he found himself reluctantly answering, "I believe he has."

"Good." She dismissed the topic abruptly.

Giving her that small bit of victory angered him. Never in his entire life had he met anyone to whom he took such an instant dislike as he did this old woman.

"Where is your granddaughter?"

The old woman smiled. *A vulture's smile.*

"She left earlier," the old bird stated.

"When do you expect her back?"

Margaret gave a noncommittal shrug. She downed her whiskey, smacking her lips in satisfaction, and poured another. She turned again to scrutinize her guest as if for the first time.

"Turn around."

"What?" he asked, confused and disoriented by her command.

"Turn around. Turn around. Are you deaf?"

Raine obeyed the absurd request, looking behind him for some possible attacker.

She smacked her lips again, obviously satisfied with more than just her whiskey. "Yes, sir. Right good-lookin'."

He had an inkling he should blush. Margaret poured the contents of yet another glass in her mouth in one quick movement, swallowing hard. But her eyes never left him.

"Can you tell me where I can find her?" His exasperation hardened his words.

"Nope."

He turned to leave, certain this trip had been in vain, and wondering where to look next for Tom's daughter. He certainly would not get a straight answer from this daft bat.

"Wait a minute!" The old woman stopped him in his tracks. "I'm not through with you yet. What is it, Raine, that you want more than anything in life?"

"That is an extremely personal question, I believe, Mrs. Carroll."

"Well, you just think about it. What would you say if I told you I would buy it for you, whatever it is? All you have to do is marry my granddaughter."

His mouth dropped open in surprise, but he immediately recovered himself.

"You would marry your granddaughter to a perfect stranger?"

"I'm a good judge of character." She shrugged and shuffled back to her chair.

"Well, obviously not if you think you can buy me. Goodbye, Mrs. Carroll." He turned once again to leave.

"Oh, don't get your dander up. She's a right nice-looking girl." She gave him a predatory smile and nodded her unconscious approval again. "Come back in two days. We'll be ready to go with you."

"We? That wasn't part of…" he began in protest.

"Be quiet," she barked, and God help him, he jumped from sheer surprise at the force and volume coming from such a small woman. "We'll all go, or no one goes." She offered him her most gracious smile, knowing she'd won the argument before it had begun.

He slammed his hat onto his head. The old woman was more than he had bargained for, but he would handle her. He would not let her think, for one minute, she had the upper hand. He tugged his hat lower on his head in an exaggerated farewell. "Very well, Mrs. Carroll. In two days, then."

Chapter Four

Millie entered her room like a forced wind, unbuttoned her jacket, and plopped herself into the corner chair. Drumming her fingers impatiently on the arm of the chair, she sat in deep contemplation. The late afternoon sun cast an oppressive, heavy heat. She swiped her sleeve across her forehead, smearing the sweat-soaked grime across it. There was no hope for it. She needed a bath. Perhaps a good soak would clear her head.

A knock on the door dissolved her deliberations for a moment.

"Come in!" she called. Gathering up her gun belt and a few other scattered belongings off the floor, she laid them on the chair where she'd been sitting as Grammie entered. The old woman looked around the room, a winsome smile on her deeply-etched face.

"I've always liked this room," she said. Millie smiled back. It had been her mother's room, and not much about it had changed, since she'd never taken it upon herself to redecorate it. She liked the feeling of being close to her mother, having never known her in any other way. It would be a pleasant reminder for Grammie.

"I'm having a bath sent up for you. I could smell you walking down the hall earlier and decided you'd forgot what they were." Grammie gave her a pointed glare, and she frowned in return.

"I was just about to start one."

"Well, let the girls bring one up for you tonight. I want to talk to you."

She usually helped the two maids prepare her bath and haul the water up the stairs to her room. She didn't like sitting around being waited on. It made her feel useless and lazy. She also wondered if Grammie would mention the stranger, and it seemed to her she showed considerable restraint by not asking about him outright.

Two young girls entered her room, each carrying buckets of steaming scalding water. Millie watched with anticipation as they poured them, one by one, into the tub. Soaking in a hot tub seemed an invitingly scrumptious diversion, but now it seemed an absolute necessity.

Her bath prepared, she undressed and lowered herself into the tub. She closed her eyes and immersed herself, luxuriating in the tingling sensation of the hot water swallowing her up.

"We had a visitor today," Grammie told her.

"Oh?" As she looked at her grandmother over the edge of the tub, she forced an air of nonchalance. She couldn't appear to be too eager. Rubbing the soap between her hands, she inhaled the sweet smell, so different from the lye bars she and Grammie usually used. Millie wondered what she'd done to deserve the luxury.

"Who was he?" she asked in a most casual tone. She sat up and scrubbed her creamy complexion until it pinkened, then leaned back again to leisurely soak, waiting for her grandmother to answer.

"If you saw him, then I'm sure you noticed he is an extremely handsome man. But I want you to stay away from him."

Millie remained quiet, choosing to weigh Grammie's words, and to not allow her disappointment to show. Millie never enjoyed being told what to do. This was the first man she'd ever looked at with any actual amount of female curiosity, and he was off-limits? Still, she kept her demeanor casual when she inquired, "Any particular reason?"

"Don't take that tone with me," her grandmother reprimanded.

"I wasn't taking a tone, Gram! Just asking a question. What's going on? Who was that man?"

"Never mind him." Grammie pulled an envelope from the breast of her dress and carefully slipped a folded paper from it. "I received this message two weeks ago." Grammie unfolded it and held out the paper to show her. Millie stuck out a wet hand to take it from her grandmother, her arm dripping water across Grammie's lap. Grammie frowned at her dress, then snatched the paper out of Millie's reach.

"I shall read it to you, so that you do not soak our only evidence," she told Millie dramatically. Grammie held up the note, which appeared to be child's work at first, a page filled with letters and words cut from the newspaper, pasted together sloppily.

As Grammie began to read the words, Millie understood her grandmother's precaution.

YOU owe mE
you will DIE if NeceSSary
I want whAT is MINE

She sat up straight in the tub. "That man sent that to you?"

"No, no. He didn't send it." Grammie shook her

head.

"But you just…Why?" Millie put her fingers to her forehead, trying to forcibly rub some patience into her brain. "Why did you tell me to stay away from him?"

"Your eyes lit up when I mentioned him. I don't want you going all simple on me. This is what we need to be focused on."

Millie sighed in resignation, too tired from trying to follow Grammie's reasoning to argue with her. She, for a moment, understood how her friend Lydia must feel. "What about the letter? Is it real?"

"It's real enough." Grammie's tone was serious, triggering Millie's guilt about losing her patience.

"Who would do something like that?" Millie's brow tensed with worry.

"I can't say for sure," Grammie hedged.

"But you have an idea?"

"Well, who was here recently sniffing around, and who might be sorely unhappy that you rejected him?"

She sifted through the theories in her head. "Parker? You can't mean that!"

"My gut instinct says, yes, that weasel, Parker Reynolds. I've known everyone in this county since I was a tot in knee britches. They're like family, and none of them would sink so low. Hell, most of them aren't smart enough to be so devious."

She couldn't argue with her grandmother's reasoning there. Parker was the only newcomer to town, until today, that is, and Parker was smart. But beyond that, he'd come across as somewhat slippery. But she hadn't wanted to acknowledge it. For a while, he'd seemed her only marriage prospect, and she'd willingly considered him. She hoped she wasn't so gullible that she might have played into his hands.

Her water cooled rapidly and feeling the toll of the day in her tired body, she'd lost the desire to indulge herself. She washed and rinsed her hair, then ringing the excess water from it, she stood and grabbed the towel hanging over Grammie's knee. Stepping out of the tub, dripping water on the worn wooden floor, she rubbed her already pink skin until it tingled. She donned the nightgown Grammie handed her, then walked over to sit on the edge of her bed. Grammie followed her and sat down next to her.

"Grammie…" She was tired and her voice was tinged with worry. "We have to do something!"

"I intend to. We'll be leaving day after tomorrow."

"Leaving? Going where?" She tried hard to decipher the overload of information swimming around in her head.

"We'll go north. We can let this business settle, and besides, don't you want to look your Pa up?"

Frowning, Millie looked over at Grammie. "He didn't want me. I don't think he'd want me suddenly showing up on his doorstep."

"You know that, do ya?" Grammie asked, a marked dent in her brow.

"Give me one reason to think otherwise," she proposed.

Grammie's face turned grim. "I won custody of you through the court," she stated matter-of-factly.

"What do you mean?"

Her grandmother sighed heavily, her shoulders drooping with her gusty exhale. "I fought your daddy for custody of you," she began, looking sideways at her granddaughter. "I could afford a better lawyer than him, that's all. That's how I came to raise you instead of him. It's not something I'm proud of, but…"

She looked at her grandmother, trying to garner the truth of her words. The severe set of her grandmother's features convinced Millie of the truth.

"You could have told me this before now." She couldn't fully comprehend the implications of Grammie's confession. She needed time to digest it.

"I didn't have the courage to," Grammie answered simply, shrugging her thin shoulders.

"But you do now?" Millie squirmed uneasily. She didn't even want to believe the man she'd spent a lifetime trying to hate might suddenly be absolved of his crimes against her.

Grammie gave her a withering look, but her voice held a sadder note, and it crackled with current. "He wanted you, Millie." Her eyes glazed over with memories as she continued. "God took my daughter, and I couldn't fight him for her. But I sure as hell could fight your Pa for the only part of her left in this world. Right or wrong, I would not let him take you away from me when he left." Her grandmother looked at her. "Don't hate me, Millie. No one could love ya more than I do."

With a mere whisper, she objected, "I could never hate you, Grammie. Don't say such a thing." She reached over and grabbed her grandmother's hand.

"Say you'll go meet him," Grammie suggested, looking at her hopefully. "It would mean everything to me to patch up all the hurt I caused you two."

Millie deliberated for a moment, her mind on the future and the possibility of meeting her father. "I'm afraid. Wyoming is so far away," she whispered.

"It wouldn't be an adventure without a little fear."

Grammie squeezed her hand with a surprising amount of strength, and scooted closer, determined to continue her plea. "What do you have to lose?"

Millie met her grandmother's expectant gaze. "I'll think about it, but you'd have to go with me. And we'd have to make arrangements for the ranch. I guess Ben could handle things on his own for a while."

"Of course I'll go with you. We'll all go. You don't think I'd let you have a grand adventure without me, do you?" Grammie asked, excitement creeping into her voice. "This will certainly rile Bridget."

Both women laughed at the idea of Bridget's turmoil, faced with the decision to stay behind alone on the ranch she loathed, or go off on a trip into wild and untamed country, far from any semblance of civilization.

Millie became pensive for a moment. Her mind wandered over the events of the day, and then she returned to a previous topic. "That man. Why was he here?"

"Your father sent him. Another thing pointing to the fact that it's time for you to meet your father. He wants you to come to him. And well, this," she held up the threatening note, "this just seals it. Besides, I sold the ranch last week to Jay Beechum, and there's nothing left to stay for." She mumbled the last sentence under her breath, so that Millie barely paid attention to it, until the words sunk in. By then, Grammie had hopped off the bed and ambled swiftly toward the doorway.

"Goodnight," Grammie offered cheerfully, as she tried to make her escape.

"Sold the ranch? This ranch? Our ranch? Without consulting me? Grammie!" She looked at the old woman, completely incensed. "How could you? We'll have nowhere to live!" She closed her eyes and massaged her temples again firmly. When she opened her eyes again to speak to Grammie, the old woman had disappeared.

"Coward!" she hissed under her breath.

She plopped down on her stomach, pulled the pillow over her head, and forced herself to think about anything other than the events that were apparently about to take place. She desperately needed some sleep. Everything would look better in the morning. It always did.

After several excruciatingly sleepless hours, she finally fell asleep, having forced herself to recall every inch of the south pasture fence. The only thing she could think of more boring than counting sheep, she often used the trick to lull herself to sleep when her mind raced. Despite being awake most of the night, Millie awoke early the next morning and was halfway down the road to town before the sun peeked over the horizon.

****

Millie rode straight into town to talk to the sheriff. But after she'd told him the details of her predicament, she had to wonder if he'd even been listening. The grotesque little lawman had dismissed her without pause. Her argument that Grammie could be in real danger fell on deaf ears. He'd sat through her story about the threatening letter and shook his head in amusement when she finished. "Your Grandmother is getting more eccentric every day." He dismissed her story with a wave of his squat, pudgy fingers.

As far as she could tell, Sheriff Smalley was a lazy, poor excuse for a lawman. He'd frustrated her beyond words, and she left his office further determined to ensure Grammie's safety.

She went to Parker's office to confront him and found it closed. His sudden disappearance incriminated him, in her mind. She'd bet he'd left town immediately following the threat on Grammie's life.

"Stupid man," she'd grumbled to no one in particular.

After reaching two dead ends, she realized she needed some professional help and sought an investigator who could find Parker's whereabouts. She had only slight reservations about the man she'd hired to investigate the threat. John "Beauty" Reichman, the burly giant she'd employed, advertised as a "private detective," but his appearance gave him the appearance of a bounty hunter.

John Reichman had a striking presence, which caused her to goose bump when he looked at her with his sharp brown eyes. Several of his teeth were possibly missing behind his tobacco; she couldn't tell, and his words were slurred and sloppy because of the enormous amount of spit he tried to contain within the wad. Several times during their conversation, he'd looked around, as if for a place to expectorate, but had held the stuff in place. This gesture, she could only assume, indicated a show of his respect, which endeared the man to her to some extent.

He smelled as if he hadn't had a bath, ever. She had a moment of doubt the wooly mammoth might ever catch up to Parker. His odor, a foul mixture of tobacco and sweat, would likely precede him, and Parker would undoubtedly smell him coming for miles. She'd love to see the expression on that coward's face when he discovered this "Beauty" looking for him. That notion made her smile.

When she'd mentioned the name Parker Reynolds, Beauty had admitted knowing him. He knew him well, in fact. She'd hesitated in telling him her story, fearing he might be a cohort of Parker's.

But then he'd asked, "What business does a fine young lady like you have with a rat bastard like him…if you'll excuse the expression?"

The "expression" had so reminded her of Grammie when he'd said it, she'd trusted him immediately and told him her problem. He appeared completely sympathetic and gave her his assurance he could accomplish the job. She'd paid him a handsome sum up-front, and he'd told her he would be in contact with her.

Thinking about John Reichman now, she couldn't be sure she hadn't made a mistake in hiring him. He was a mystery and little of a loner. However, she couldn't rest until she could confront Parker, and she couldn't do that until she found him.

By midmorning, her stomach rumbled ravenously. She entered the hotel lobby and looked around. The only hotel for many miles, it had been grand in its day. However, signs of wear were now apparent on the old building and decor. Faded landscapes adorned the wallpaper, the paper itself chipped and peeling, and the worn carpets showed its age. Still, the hotel was clean and well managed. The big bay windows filled the room with sunshine, and the richness of the plush, ornate furnishings, even though several decades old, made the building seem grand.

As she walked into the dining room, there were several people scattered about. Seating herself at an isolated table by a window, she ordered and chatted lightly with the serving girl. The girl departed, and she glanced over both shoulders to see who she could see, hoping to spot Parker.

Her eyes landed on the stranger from yesterday, seated alone in the corner. To her chagrin, he stared right back at her. She blushed under his intense stare. He gave a slight bow of his head to her, and she looked away.

Self-consciously, she unfolded her napkin and placed it in her lap, waiting for her breakfast to arrive. After what seemed an eternity, she turned again and caught his gaze.

Though he seemed not to think twice about her misplaced curiosity, she was relieved when someone stepped in between them, giving her a target for her attention.

The young cowboy standing in front of her had worked for her and Grammie for several summers. Covered with a thick layer of dirt from his neck down, but with a face wiped shiny clean, he offered her a shy smile. He gripped his hat in both hands. He was a hard worker, and Millie genuinely liked him, so she smiled at him in greeting.

"Good morning, Tyler." She indicated the chair across from her, offering him a seat, but he declined with a hesitant shake of his head.

"Just stopped by to say hello."

He stood there, wringing his hat like a small child, as if he wanted to say more.

"Was there something else?" she whispered.

"Well, yes, ma'am. I wondered if you knew that man behind you?"

Millie didn't have to look around. "The one in the corner?"

Tyler nodded. "He's been staring at you. I thought

at first that maybe he knowed you, but when you turned around, you didn't say anything. If you want me to say somethin' to him…"

It seemed a gallant offer, but if he could barely summon the courage to speak a "good morning" to her, she had to wonder where he would find it to give the stranger, who happened to be twice and a half his size, a good dressing down for impolitely staring.

"Thank you, Ty. I do appreciate it. I believe he knows my grandmother, that's all. And I'm sure he didn't even realize he was staring."

His shoulders relaxed as he smiled. He nodded his head in farewell, turned, and ran to catch up with his friends.

Perhaps the stranger knew her identity. Why else would he stare at her? She should introduce herself. After all, he was a friend of her father's, sent down here because of her. It would be downright rude to ignore him. Taking her napkin from her lap, she hesitantly placed it on the table, scooted out her chair, and gathered her courage. "He's just a man," she told herself, pushing away from the table.

As she drew near him, walking with all the confidence she usually possessed but didn't at the moment, she briefly studied his appearance. His clothes were clean and of high quality, not typical for a cowboy, but he stood out for other reasons as well. With his coal black hair, striking, silver-blue eyes framed by dark, thick eyelashes, full lips over white teeth, there could be no doubt what qualifications Grammie perceived in him. And seeing him up close unsettled her to an even greater extent, but she found her tongue somehow.

"Hello," she offered nervously, extending her hand

and bestowing on him a warm smile. "I'm Millie." For a girl who took pride in her inability to be intimidated, she found her courage had easily escaped her.

His gaze swept over her from top to bottom, embarrassing her with its blatant scrutiny. He extended his arm and shook her offered hand. She observed the warmth, the roughness, the largeness of it, and a mysterious heat seeped through her. She noted with dismay the blush stealing up her neck as she waited for him to acknowledge their connection.

"A pleasure." Her boldness obviously amused him. Sitting back casually in his chair, he draped one arm over the back of it as he regarded her. "You know, with the sun shining through that window, it looked like your entire head had caught fire. Remarkable."

He'd been staring at her hair? Surely, he teased, but nothing in his expression indicated humor. He didn't know her identity, that much was clear. When she merely stood there with a questioning frown, he raised an eyebrow. She felt like a fool as he sat there staring at her, his arrogance prickling like a bur under her saddle blanket.

Then suddenly he smiled at her, and it struck her dumb, before she realized that due to her lack of anything to say, she was the source of his amusement.

Whirling around in a fluster, she bumped into a cart, which had definitely not been there before. The mound of dirty dishes it held clashed to the floor, like an orchestra of symbols resounding in an empty concert hall. She scrambled to halt the flow of silverware over the side of the cart.

Then his deep voice came from behind her, silky and deceptive. "Are you okay?"

Curbing the impulse to break into a dead run toward the nearest door out of sheer humiliation, she straightened, ignoring the silverware which still fell from the cart like a trickling waterfall. She wiped her hands down the legs of her jeans, more to steady herself than because they were soiled.

"If you're in town looking for work," she offered, looking over her shoulder at the handsome, slack-jawed stranger frozen halfway out of his chair in alarm, "I think you could get on here as a dishwasher. They seem to be short on help."

Walking as calmly as possible back to her table, she sat and unfolded her napkin again with painful deliberation, placing it and smoothing it across her lap. Her breakfast awaited, but the encounter had ruined her appetite. She could only stare at the grease-laden plate of eggs and bacon now on the table in front of her. "Of all the cussed fools," she muttered under her breath, not sure if her anger was toward him or at herself.

A large form appeared and loomed somewhere to her side. She feared the handsome stranger stood waiting for her to look his way. *Please go away.*

Finally, she looked up at him. Offering her a smile, which to her, seemed more of a wince than an actual smirk, he tipped his hat and walked away. She watched him go out, watched his manly swagger through the lobby and down the sidewalk, and she sighed.

Well, Grammie, for once you were right. I should have stayed far away from him.

Chapter Five

Raine arrived at the old woman's ranch by dawn the next day, ready to start the arduous journey home. He did not look forward to it. If he could simply ride straight home, he could probably have enjoyed the travel, but the miles of wilderness, in combination with one bratty heiress and one senile old woman, did not constitute the ingredients of a pleasurable trip. God, who was he kidding? Tom's daughter was even worse than he'd imagined. When the old woman had introduced him to Bridget this morning, it first struck him that she was pretty, at least she probably would be when she awoke fully, and the sleepiness had left her puffy face. But it didn't take him long to realize that was where the positive attributes ended.

Spoiled, brazenly forward, and extremely rude were the descriptions that came to mind. And the old woman, well, he could never have imagined her. She was worse than Tom had described her, and he'd not imagined that possible. If dealing with all of that wasn't bad enough, he would begin the trip without so much as even a few hours of sleep.

Retiring early, he'd intended to have a good night's sleep, grateful it was his last night in this sweltering hot hotel room. He'd hoped sleep would wipe out the image of a certain feminine body in men's britches, but he realized early into the evening she'd planted herself there. His initial attraction to her irked him. It wasn't without reason. She was beautiful, in a way, though compelling might be more precise, with her silky, auburn curls, her shapely derriere accentuated by those snug pants. She'd affected him with those sharp green eyes and that mass of red hair. Regardless, she was young, clumsy at that, and being attracted to her made him a reprobate. Gladly, he'd never see her again.

Retiring to his room early, he'd stripped himself naked, his only defense against the humid Kansas night, and settled himself face down atop his less than comfortable bed. But sleep had eluded him, and he'd lain awake for most of the night listening to someone in the next room banging around. Even a pillow held tightly over his head hadn't drowned out the noise next door or the images of the girl. But he could no longer stew over his loss of sleep, because the quirky little entourage would leave within an hour. Once they were on the trail, and he could throw his blanket under a starry, ink-black night sky, he would sleep.

He cursed that idea now as he checked his gear one last time, knowing they had a hard day of travel ahead before he'd find any comfort in his bedroll. Another cup of coffee would help him face the day. What would it hurt? They could leave now or ten hours from now. It really didn't matter. He was destined for hell, and no matter how he tried to convince himself he'd make it through, he couldn't shake the dread of events he couldn't possibly predict or comprehend.

The early morning light barely broke as he went back to the old woman's house for more coffee. He stood on the porch and looked at the horizon to estimate how much time he had till sunup. The house was quiet, not because they were asleep, but because they scurried around like mice raiding the kitchen at night, quietly going about their business, as if it were illegal to be up at this hour. At least the coffee was strong, and for the time being, he cared about little else.

As he turned to go inside, resigning himself to make the best of an intolerable situation, and reminding himself he'd volunteered to do this, the screen door suddenly swung open and smacked him hard on the nose.

"Damn," he barked, his curse slicing through the quiet of pre-dawn obscenely. A woman's faint gasp sounded in the darkness, but he couldn't see into the dark recess of the entry.

"Oh!"

When his eyes stopped watering, and he could open them enough to see who had assaulted him, he pulled open the screen, hoping to catch the perpetrator before she escaped, but the hall was empty. Massaging the bridge of his stinging nose, he went to the kitchen with all the enthusiasm of a man walking to his own execution.

Both the old woman and Bridget were there. Both looked up at him curiously, and he scowled at them.

"Coffee?" Margaret croaked.

Obviously, no one intended to own up to almost breaking his nose, so he sighed and pulled up a chair across from Bridget.

"Yes, please." Then, in an attempt at conversation, he spoke to Bridget. "Your father is certainly looking forward to meeting you."

She rolled her eyes. An odd response to Raine's way of thinking, and in an exchange he didn't wholly understand, the old woman gave Bridget a withering look, causing her to perk up and smile. Her pretty smile took him aback, but it seemed unnatural somehow.

"I'm really looking forward to meeting him, too. All these years…" She let the sentence hang dramatically, and Raine took a sip of coffee so he didn't have to respond. It would be a long trip.

Margaret put a plate of eggs and sausage in front of him, which he gratefully accepted. "Thank you," he said, as she pulled a chair out to sit next to him. She pinned him with those great, bulging eyes, and he felt like a schoolboy in trouble. He proceeded to eat, knowing this would be his last meal for hours, and he waited patiently for whatever she wanted to say. Meanwhile, he chewed, self-consciously, on eggs with the consistency of wet leather. He didn't know whether he should swallow them or spit the chewed-up remains out and fashion a pair of moccasins. Either way, the breakfast did little to satisfy his desire for a home-cooked meal.

Having swallowed as many bites of eggs as he could justify, he bit into his toast, which tasted reasonably good due to the generous slathering of butter atop it and washed it down with warm milk. He finished the toast with a second bite and noisily pushed his chair away from the table, moving himself out of the direct line of two sets of probing eyeballs. He thanked Margaret for the breakfast, told the two women he'd make sure their belongings were secured to their wagon, and if they were ready, they could be leaving within the hour. And so he escaped.

He walked out the back of the house, stepping onto the dry, sandy dirt, and checked the horizon for the time once again, knowing the sun would soon pop over the horizon and smother him with its heat. Scanning the wagon's contents to ascertain the security of their belongings, Raine saw a movement in the corner of his eye.

There paced a dog, he assumed, although it looked like a wolf, back and forth in front of the barn door. The creature eyed him warily, stopping his pacing only long enough to determine Raine's interest in him. It was a scraggly creature at best, but obviously tame. Raine's curiosity was piqued. He'd heard of people taming wolves, raising them from pups. Apparently, they made loyal pets once domesticated. He couldn't imagine either Bridget or Margaret having any interest in such endeavors, so he supposed the animal belonged to the ranch hand, Ben.

The notion of Ben accompanying them gave Raine a sense of slight relief. He would not be the sole ringleader of this circus. Ben had obviously been with Margaret for many years and would therefore know how to handle the eccentric old coot. Ben would travel with them at Margaret's suggestion. Actually, it had been the first suggestion the woman had made he'd agreed with, and perhaps because of it, this trip wouldn't be as dreadful as he'd feared.

****

Millie woke in a cross mood, prepared to tell Grammie she would not take part in this fiasco. She'd told her how she'd met the man her father had hired, had determined he was rude and contemptible, and finally that she would not travel to heaven, to hell, or even to Wyoming with him.

Grammie decreed that this man, Raine, be kept in the dark about Millie's identity. Millie failed to see how this saved her from his company, but Grammie assured her if he believed Bridget was her father's daughter, and the heir apparent to her fortune, he'd be so busy falling over himself to please her, he wouldn't even notice Millie. That scenario prickled her ire exceedingly.

As far as Bridget went, well, she didn't care what she had to do to get away from the ranch; she simply wanted out. Grammie explained that her opportunity had arrived. If she went along with her scheme, Grammie promised to set her up in Denver, with a chaperone, of course, in her own place. Grammie would give her an allowance, and she could live comfortably in a city, just as she'd always dreamed.

Bridget surely did not know why Grammie wanted her to pretend to be Thomas McConnell's daughter, but she most likely didn't care. The promise of Denver would be impossible for her to refuse.

Frankly, Millie didn't understand the reasoning behind the ruse either. Grammie saw every man as a potential fortune hunter, and perhaps she thought by diverting his attention to Bridget, Millie would be safe from his attentions. Whatever the reason, just as Bridge couldn't refuse Denver, she couldn't refuse the chance to meet her father.

Regardless of her reasons, Grammie had already introduced Bridge as "the daughter", and since she'd not been named until after her father had left, the lie held. That man had no reason to question Bridget's identity, and therefore, did not. If she came out and told the truth now, they would all come across as a bunch of loonies before the trip even began. No, it would be better to wait until they were well under way before he found out what an utterly insane bunch they truly were.

Lord, but things didn't bode well for her so far. The first day of the trip—they hadn't even started traveling yet, and she'd already nearly knocked him out with the door. If he'd known it was her, he would surely think her the clumsiest female ever, and she just didn't think she could ever face him again. Hopefully, he'd not seen her. Heaven knows, she'd not seen him standing there in the dark. After she'd whacked him, she'd run up the steps two at a time and hid in the safety of her room. She would have to give him a wide berth. But for now, she had to finish her preparations for leaving. She had everything she needed for the ride packed in her saddlebags, but a few small personal items were still in her room.

A fleeting sense of sentiment filled her. Grammie had decorated the room in yellow, lavender, and lace. Hand-stitched dolls her grandmother had made many years ago filled the room. It was a young girl's room, her mother's, but Millie had never wanted to change it. Her Grammie had obviously put a great deal of love and pride in preparing it.

She went to the pine chest under the window, threw off the patchwork pillows stacked on top, and opened the lid. Pushing aside several dime novels, she carefully reached in and pulled out an ornate silver box. It contained some of her parent's possessions, and she cherished it as her only link to the mother and father she'd never known. She ran her hand lightly over the top and opened it. The items it contained were familiar: the locket with portraits of both her mother and father, a broach her father had made and given to her mother on the day of their wedding, a thimble, a pipe with dried tobacco still in the bowl, a lace collar, a lock of brown hair, some worthless coins. The personal items never failed to stir fantasies of her parents.

Lost in such visions, Millie gently touched the stem of the pipe, then closed the box. Tucking it away under her arm, she snuck downstairs, and slipped out the front, mindful not to let the screen door slam behind her. She walked out to the stables to secure the box with the rest of her things. As she walked, she lovingly reached down to scratch Jack on the scruff of his neck, as he followed close on her heels.

While she checked her saddle and secured her belongings, Jack suddenly leapt from his position at her side and walked to the front of the barn. He'd obviously spied someone. She could tell by the way he paced back and forth. He was a loyal companion and extremely wary of others. She unconsciously caressed the Colt at her side and peeked out the door. In the early dawn she was virtually invisible inside the dark barn. She recognized Raine again. She'd know that distinct black hair, coupled with those broad, muscular shoulders, anywhere.

She watched him eyeing Jack, but not with the usual wariness that people had toward her wolf. He then returned to his task of securing the trunks to Grammie's wagon.

Millie considered all that they were leaving behind. Grammie had no qualms about leaving a good portion of her belongings and intended to only take her most valuable things.

She had the feeling Grammie viewed this trip as an exciting adventure. She seemed thrilled at the idea of the new beginning, and Millie had to admit, her enthusiasm was contagious. The concept of starting completely fresh, going into the unknown, discovering new places, meeting new people, did excite Millie. She liked to see her grandmother looking forward to starting over, as well, instead of waiting for the end of her life. Grammie's mindset prevented Millie from arguing with her about this whole affair.

She kept her eye on the man who would be their guardian for the trip. He checked the security of the trunks, then the wagon itself, pushing against it to test the sturdiness and checking each wheel in turn. When he finished the job, obviously satisfied with the results, he strolled away.

Millie left the dark safety of the stable and followed. If she were careful and took her time, he'd never know she was watching him. She snuck around the corner of the corncrib. He crouched on his knees, digging in the dirt by the gate of the family cemetery. Quietly, she walked up behind him. Diligently, he continued scooping dirt.

The day heated rapidly as the early morning sun made its appearance above the horizon. The muscles played across his back through the sweat-soaked shirt as he dug, and she trailed a drop of sweat with her eyes as it ran from his hairline down his neck, disappearing beneath his shirt collar. She bit her lip. She'd watched men work and sweat her entire life, but never had the sight of one played such havoc with her insides. Her heart quickened its pace as her insides churned with an alien sensation.

Having already dug a considerable hole, he adjusted to the right, scratching the surface of a new one.

"Looking for anyone in particular?" Millie asked suspiciously.

He froze, then sat back on his haunches. Resting one arm on his knee, he turned and looked back at her, confusion marring his expression. Scowling, he stood and slapped his hands on his pants, sending clouds of dust into the air.

"What the hell!" he barked.

Obviously, he didn't feel the need to explain himself. She put her hands on her hips and shot back, "'What the hell' what?"

He gave her form a vertical perusal. Cocking his head, he looked at her accusingly. "Did you follow me here?"

The look of disbelief on her face should have been enough to convince him she hadn't, but when he raised an eyebrow at her, still waiting for an answer, she could see it wasn't. She wouldn't demean herself by answering such a ridiculously vain question. She turned to the house and left him standing there.

****

He watched her go, wondering where exactly she would go. When she walked through the back door of the house, he realized she somehow belonged in this group of screwballs. Frankly, he didn't want to know. The last thing he needed was her in the mix of this trip. A woman had no right to wear pants like a man, not when she filled them out so effectively. It was indecent, stirring as hell, but indecent, just the same. She had freckles, though only a light splattering, and a mass of unruly curls the color of earth and fire…What on earth was he thinking?

Raine stood for a moment, shaking his head to clear it. Looking heavenward, he went down on his knees to continue his search. She wasn't exactly the type he would imagine himself being attracted to, but damned if he wasn't. At least she wouldn't be travelling to Wyoming with them. He hoped.

After digging only a few inches deeper, he hit something solid, the box containing the ancient bottle of Scots whiskey Tom had told him to find. Gently, he pulled it from the ground, and after inspecting it, wrapped it in cloth. He briefly wondered what kind of eccentricity led a woman to bury her valuables in the family cemetery. What other things still might be buried, also of some value, that the old woman had simply forgotten about? He walked to his horse to secure the bottle away in his saddlebag.

Ben walked up behind him with the two horses he'd selected for the trip. They were fine quarter horses, as good as any he'd seen. The two men worked side by side, silently finishing their tasks. When the horses were hitched and ready, the two men stood and faced each other. Ben nodded, as if to acknowledge they worked well together. Raine agreed, nodding his confirmation, grateful to have an ally in this parade of fools.

"I'll get the women," Ben turned toward the house. Raine had doubts as to whether Ben would be good company. The man didn't exactly overflow with words. It didn't matter. He was going home, and he cared about little else. Twenty minutes later, the women emerged from the house. He gratefully noted the absence of the redhead.

Waiting for them by the horses, a clean white shirt, and his mood improved, he helped Margaret into her wagon. He paused. "Did you pack warmer clothes? There will be snow by the time we reach the mountains. And considerably colder temperatures."

"I packed my coat," she said.

"Yes, well, you'll need some gear in addition to that," he told her gently. "It's a different climate, but we'll stop and make sure you're both outfitted properly." He fussed over them the exact amount of time he believed appropriate to make them feel fussed over, feeling charitable and noble in his efforts, bestowed on them a rare smile, and turned away, adjusting his hat over his hair.

He'd considered it while he'd waited on them to join him, and he'd figured out the way to handle this whole impossible situation. It would only take a little charm. He had these two well in hand. What had he been so worried about? They were just women, after all. He climbed atop his own horse and took his reins in hand. He urged his mount forward. "Let's go, then."

He looked back at the wagon, deciding to give the women another smile for good measure, when he noticed the old woman looking back at the house. *Having second thoughts*, he mused silently. He didn't blame her. She was brave for leaving her home at such an old age, and he admired her spunk. But suddenly, for some reason, the fact that she repeatedly turned and stared at the house gave him pause.

An hour later, when the house disappeared completely from sight, and she still kept looking backward, he scanned the horizon himself. He looked for something of interest there, but nothing appeared. It was the most uneventful horizon he'd ever seen. Soon he turned to scan the landscape periodically with a prickly feeling he knew what to expect. Why had the redhead walked into the old woman's house like she lived there, and if she did live there, why would she be left there alone?

He could no longer contain his curiosity. He pulled up his reins, turning his horse, and fell in beside the wagon containing the two women.

"Mrs. Carroll," he began.

"Margaret, please."

"Margaret. Will there be anyone else joining us?" he asked simply.

She appeared to appreciate his astuteness, but she didn't answer him. She deliberately ignored his question.

"Who's the girl? Is she a relative of yours?"

"She is my other granddaughter. And yes, she's coming with us." At his frown, she continued, "You don't have to worry about her. She can take care of herself. And she'll catch up when she's ready." She dismissed him by closing her eyes and immediately pretending to sleep.

He rode ahead with a considerable frown, a little perturbed at the news. The old woman should have given him this information long before now. He rubbed his forehead, regretting for about the one-hundredth time agreeing to this escort. He eagerly anticipated the moment his job ended, he could be rid of these women, and he could get back to the business of ranching.

Looking around him, he hoped he'd never have reason to see Kansas again. He could appreciate the simple beauty of it all, but he didn't think he'd ever be able to adapt to the humidity. He wondered how the women would adapt to the mountains of Wyoming. No doubt like fish take to pine trees.

Chapter Six

Grammie, Bridge, Ben, and Raine settled for the night just at dusk, leaving little time for the setting up of an elaborate camp. By the time Millie crept up just out of sight to spy on the small group, they had a fire going and were putting up a tent for Grammie and Bridge. She held back from the group for a while, not wanting another confrontation with Raine. She'd never met a man who wreaked such havoc with her insides when he looked at her. She doubted herself. That was an alien sensation, and until she could come to terms as to why he caused this upheaval, she intended to keep her distance. Still, her stomach had a hole in it, and since she'd been sitting there, Grammie had returned to the fire several times, obviously preparing a meal. She'd eaten all that she'd brought with her, which had been little. She'd have to join them, and soon. The acrid smell of smoke wafted across the distance. The biscuits would be rising in the Dutch oven. Maybe beef on the spit. Beans. Beans would be good.

She walked in, leading her horse behind her, and nearly jumped out of her skin at the deep masculine voice suddenly behind her. "From now on, stay with the rest of us. I'm not here to pamper spoiled little girls, and I have enough to worry about without you wandering around alone. If you're traveling with us, you're under my care, and you'll do as I say." Raine walked away, leaving

Millie red-faced and angry, like a balloon that had just unexpectedly been popped. She'd never taken orders from a man in her life, which presented a dilemma.

Somewhere along the way, she'd decided she would stay with the group, having spent the day alone, hot, hungry, and bored. But now if she stayed, he'd think he intimidated her. She mounted her horse and rode out of camp, still hungry, but urged by the knowledge that Raine would be angry at being ignored. She wouldn't ride out far, though. She wasn't stupid. There were still many dangers on a night like this, rattlers being foremost in her mind. She had a deathly fear of the blasted things. She weaved back and forth, not traveling far from the group, for about a half an hour.

Unconsciously, she slowed as she considered being out there in the dark alone. She couldn't build a fire without drawing attention to herself and causing Raine to seek her out and humiliate her further. The night air had already begun to cool, and she also didn't relish the idea of laying down her bedroll and having some varmint crawl in with her, seeking warmth. It had been known to happen, with disastrous results for the occupant of the bedroll. She could take some comfort that Jack would sleep with her and alert her to any danger, but would it be soon enough?

She could see next to nothing, except the fire a short distance away, which looked warm and inviting, making the area around its circle of light even darker and colder. She slapped the reins against her leg. Those people were her family. He, the outsider, should be the one uncomfortable in their camp, not her. She had every right to be there. But if she went back, he'd win, though only the one battle, she told herself. She could allow him that.

She dismounted and walked toward the camp. Perhaps his only concern was her welfare. But he'd think her a fool, not brave, if she stayed out here and put herself in danger for no reason other than pride.

Raine smirked when he spied her. She sat down next to Grammie and accepted the plate Ben offered.

Even better than she'd expected, the plate of scrumptious stew steamed with hot gravy as it spread over a split biscuit. She dug into the meal with fervor, eating the huge helping in six or seven bites. She stood and helped herself to another helping. Satisfied with the heaping amount on her plate, she sat down and indulged herself again in the delicious stew. Feeling full, almost uncomfortably so, she put her plate on the ground for Jack, who was just finishing up someone else's meager scraps. She straightened her back, stretching her torso to allow room in her full belly. Feeling the heavy weight of someone's stare, she turned to find Raine watching her with something akin to amazement on his face.

"What?" she asked. He shook his head, as if to dismiss his judgements before he could voice them and turned and walked away.

She refrained from pulling a face at his back. Stroking Jack's neck affectionately, she absently pondered why her father's man affected her so adversely. When she looked at him, something unpleasant snaked through her, though she didn't entirely recognize it yet. Resentment? Yes. Embarrassment? Yes. Hatred? Hopefully. Desire? Hopefully not. Curiosity? Most definitely. She was curious about him. She couldn't deny that.

Grammie started suddenly, snorting as she did, and Millie realized the old woman had been dozing. No wonder she'd been so quiet. "Can I help you to bed, Grammie?"

Margaret shook her head no, but Millie stood to help her stand. Linking her arm through her grandmother's, she walked with her the short distance to her tent. Bridge slept, indicated by the loud snoring from inside. Millie pecked her Grammie on the cheek, then sent her inside. Knowing there would be a stack of dirty dishes by the wash pan, she turned to the task of cleaning up.

In a dark area just beyond camp where the horses were hobbled, Ben and Raine talked quietly, the lighted ends of their cheroots glowing in the dark. How she envied their freedom. She'd like nothing other than to be over there talking to a friend, enjoying the night air and a good smoke. She'd never actually tried cigars, but men could smoke without reproach, and it wasn't fair. Finishing up the dishes and drying her hands on a towel lying handy, she strained to hear what the men talked about, but could only discern the low rumble of their voices across the night air, nothing to indicate any actual words. Unrolling her own bedroll, she placed it as close to the fire as she could. Having taken care of her necessities earlier, she immediately crawled into her bed and stared up at the stars, feeling her body melt into the hard earth underneath her.

She fell asleep almost immediately. The next moment, a booted toe nudging her backside brought her from the depths of slumber. Groggy and disoriented, she rolled over to discover Raine glowering down at her.

"You," he stated, as if that were her name, "sleep in the tent."

"No." Dismissing him, she rolled back over.

He jerked off her covers. "Come on. Get up. The

women sleep in the tent. The men sleep out here."

Her frown took a sharp turn downward as she stood to face him, lifting her chin in defiance. "I'm not sleeping in the tent. You can't make me."

He turned her around and pushed her toward the tent, brooking no arguments. As they neared, a loud grinding noise, emanating from the tent, assaulted his ears. He stopped, with Millie in front of him, and dropped his hands to his side. "What the hell is that?" he asked.

"That," she informed him, as she turned to look at him, "is called snoring. And it keeps me awake. You can't make me go in there."

He hesitated a moment, looking down into a pool of sea-green eyes, lit by the flicker of the campfire, and the slight spattering of freckles across the bridge of her nose. "No, I don't suppose I can." He smiled, despite his best intentions not to. Chuckling softly, he asked conspiratorially, "Who is it?'

The smile made her falter only a little. "Decency prohibits me from revealing the source, but let me assure you that lying in the same room with her will ruin any hope of a good night's sleep. Good night." She sidestepped him and returned to her bedroll.

He watched her go, all of her, then looked back at the tent from where the hideously loud snoring came. Shaking his head in disbelief, he walked to his horse and removed his own bedroll. He placed it in the only spot available next to the fire and lay down. The wolf watched him unwaveringly. It would probably bite him first chance if it took after his master.

When Raine opened his eyes the next morning, Millie still slept across from him. The fire had died, but the dawn's first light crept into the sky. Millie lay in almost the same position he'd last seen her before he fell asleep. She appeared to be a sound sleeper, but there was evidence she'd tossed and turned. He lay still, watching her, enjoying the warmth of his bedroll for just a moment longer. Her face was delicate and well-formed, and her hair a mass of dark red curls framing her pretty face. Her mouth hung open a little, and a small puddle of drool ran from her lips and pooled on her hands, where they rested in a praying position beneath her cheek. She certainly didn't look like the fearsome creature she seemed to think herself. She looked like a glowing angel, asleep there across from him—a drooling, glowing angel.

Sluggishly, her eyes fluttered opened, and she looked directly into his. Sitting up suddenly, she wiped the back of her sleeve across her mouth and blinked hard several times, unaware of him. Raine sat up, too, and watched as she struggled to get her bearings.

"Good morning," he whispered.

She replied with a confused, questioning grunt as she looked around, then over at him again, almost cross-eyed.

She then looked around her as if to sum up the situation. Her hair fell loose from its braid, wild and twice the size it had been the day before. Raine's amusement caused him to halfheartedly poke at the fire as he watched her. When she stood, at first unsteadily, the wolfdog instantly jumped to her side. She smiled down at him in recognition and scratched him behind the ear.

There was a moment of awkwardness, as they were the only two awake. She went out of her way to ignore him, but whenever he caught her looking at him, her eyes contained a small amount of horror. She tugged at the curls hanging over her eyes, realizing her disheveled state and embarrassed at having been caught in a less than flattering situation. He had tried to prevent this last night.

Hoping to use this to his advantage, he turned to her with a condescending, fatherly expression. "It is awkward, us being strangers and sleeping right across from each other. Why don't you reconsider sleeping in the tent from now on?"

"I can see why you'd be embarrassed!" she exclaimed in a loud whisper. "Have you always snored like that, or did you break your nose in a saloon brawl or something? I've never heard such God-awful braying, even from the scroungiest and most exhausted of cowboys. You're even worse than Bridge. How do you sleep through it?" She shook her red head in disgust at him. "I think it is you who should consider setting up a tent for yourself, putting a pillow over your head. Give the rest of us the chance to catch some winks. What a racket!"

Raine found himself speechless. No one had ever accused him of snoring, and here this strange creature had done just that. She didn't even realize he'd tried to reproach her. She'd just blasted into him with her insults, leaving him standing there as confused as if he'd just been hit in the head and lost his wits. He laughed bitterly in disbelief. Oh, well. So much for using intimidation as a tactic to handle that one.

Ben soon stirred and the three of them worked together to gather fuel for the fire, make coffee, and prepare a light breakfast of biscuits and eggs. Raine glanced occasionally at Millie and frowned when she shook her head at him, as if disgusted by his defect.

Margaret and Bridget were late in waking up, and on this first morning, Raine wouldn't rush them. A sense of urgency about getting home compelled him, but he wouldn't take away any slight comfort the women might find. He intended to allow them a leisurely breakfast and time for their daily necessities. This trip would be hard on them, especially the old woman. Hurrying would only make it especially so. He could set a pace, once in motion, to make up for any slight loss of time. It was uncharacteristic of him to give allowance to others, especially ones he disliked as much as he did this bunch. Still, they were women, and Bridget was Tom's daughter.

When the old woman finally emerged from her tent, she walked toward the small group, her eyebrows raised in question over her bug eyes, and a queer smile on her lips. She raised her small chin, peered down her nose through her thick spectacles, looked the three of them over closely, then asked, "So? How'd ya' sleep?"

"Awful," Millie answered instantly, with what Raine believed some amount of exaggeration. He frowned at her again, but otherwise refused to comment on how he'd slept. Ben answered, however, only because Margaret's full attention fell now on him.

"I slept great." His words carried a note of apology, sitting between Raine and Mille scowling at each other.

Bridget emerged soon after that with a considerable frown marring her usually pretty features. She sat down among them, slack-mouthed and dazed. All at once, she screwed up her face and started bawling. She made squeaking, chirping noises, which she tried to pass off as speech. He understood little of what she uttered, but he deciphered the sequence of words which showed her concern for being forced to rise early every morning for the rest of the trip. Margaret, Millie, and even Ben circled around her in a gesture of comfort. Raine felt a good swift kick to the backside might be the better approach, but he refrained from mentioning it.

The entire scene being beyond what he could bear, he walked away without explanation and set about breaking down and packing up the temporary camp. The sooner he could be home, the better. Comforts be damned.

Chapter Seven

As they neared Colorado, Millie didn't know if she was going to shoot her grandmother, her escort, or herself, but she would be shooting somebody. Shooting her unpredictable grandmother seemed to hold the most merit at the moment, but she'd like to shoot Raine just for the principle of it. Shooting herself would be a last-minute act of mercy.

The situation, as she surmised it, was that Raine hated her and used every aspect of his authority to make her miserable. Grammie really had lost her mind, and on alternating days, faked an illness: a stroke, a sprained ankle, temporary blindness. These spells caused Raine, in his own moments of lunacy, to jump at the slightest show of pain from Grammie, despite his obvious distaste for the old faker.

At first, Grammie's failing health alarmed Millie too, and she also bounded to Grammie's side, usually causing Millie to butt heads with Raine. It took Millie three or four of these run-ins to realize she' played into Grammie's well-planned out drama, and that Grammie's health was, in fact, intact. Millie could not decipher Grammie's intentions, save for the fact that she basked in the attention, but she didn't intend to fall for it again.

Raine must have also realized the old woman's health remained steady, because after a while, he wouldn't go near Grammie. Instead, he put Ben in charge of seeing to her needs. Ben, being a much better sport about the whole affair, took Grammie's bellyaching and cross nature with secret amusement. But then he and Grammie had long ago forged a relationship built on shared mischievousness.

Grammie clearly enjoyed herself, as evidenced by the twinkle of laughter in her eye. Millie wasn't so lucky. The trip had been harder than she'd anticipated, because Raine drove them at an unmerciful pace. Since Grammie and Bridget were incapable, or unwilling, to help in any meaningful way, Mille had to pick up the slack as far as tending horses, setting up camp, cleaning up after meals, packing up for Grammie and Bridget, and setting up and taking down camp. She didn't dare complain, no matter how exhausted she became. She imagined Raine pushed them at this pace just to see her give in and admit it exhausted her. She intended to prove he had much to learn about Millie McConnell.

Millie reckoned he had much to learn about women in general. He threw an open challenge in Millie's face and expected her to back down. Grammie totally flabbergasted him, and Bridge, of all people, he tried to pamper and coddle. The more he tried to please her, the more attention she demanded. Millie had to admit his attention to Bridget disappointed her. She shouldn't have cared. But she did.

After almost two weeks of putting up with their nonsense, Raine had avoided all of them for several days, not that she could blame him. Relieved she hadn't had to deal with his unpleasant demeanor, she'd tried not to think of him at all. It only created a restlessness in her gut. She didn't like it and didn't understand the reason for it. But honestly, there was little else to think about while traveling such a long stretch. Thankfully, they would make camp early today, which meant she would be too busy to think of anything or anyone.

They stopped near a small creek. The quiet spot came alive with a flurry of activity as the men began setting up camp. A current of excitement seemed to flow through the small group as everyone prepared for a small respite from the grueling pace Raine had set for them. Millie, too, appreciated the break as she helped unload food from the wagon for dinner.

As things settled down a bit, she spotted Raine, and not for the first time ashamedly experienced a wave of pleasure she couldn't understand in the least. Except for being pleasing to look at, he had to be the most unpleasant man she'd ever met. She couldn't help but wonder if his attitude towards her would change if he knew her true identity. That concept made her further determined to play out the charade in which she'd become entangled.

Raine and Ben were immersed in conversation when he caught her eye, and she blushed at having been caught staring at him. He held her gaze for a moment before he frowned and turned away. Millie sighed heavily. Did he always frown, or did he save them all for her? Suddenly feeling vastly alone, she decided to spend some time with Grammie and Bridge. It would feel good to talk with them like they were still at home, and she hadn't left everything behind. Feeling as if her bones weighed a ton, she stood and took a few steps towards where Grammie stood hunched over her stew.

Looking back over her shoulder at Raine, she faltered. She'd become accustomed to her desire to look at him. She'd accepted the fact that seeing him quickened her heartbeat and caused a stirring deep within her. True, he was a feast for the eyes, but without the proper soul, what good was a man? She didn't know what kind of soul he possessed, and frankly, she didn't care, because her woman's curiosity had been so aroused by his nearness, she could give some allowance that he may not be a saint. She only wanted a piece of him.

If she could only get to know him, perhaps she would find him arrogant and vile. She had faith in her own moral sense and judgment, and she wasn't simple enough to throw caution to the wind, just because the sight of him had to be close to heaven on earth. But what if he turned out to be a good sort? What would become of these fierce cravings brewing inside of her? And what if, after knowing him, and truly liking him, he scorned her, leaving her wanting what she couldn't have? This cyclone of feeling inside of her had become a terrible mess. But the storm existed, none the less. She couldn't deny it.

She looked up to find Grammie staring at her hard. "Wool-gathering?"

"I'm afraid so."

Grammie knowingly followed Raine with her eyes as he walked out of camp and reached over, placing her rough hand over Millie's. She gave it a slight squeeze, saying nothing but understanding everything. Millie blushed, realizing nothing, not even her most guarded emotions, escaped the old woman. Hopefully, Grammie didn't understand the full extent of her thinking.

"Where's Bridge?" Millie asked her grandmother. An afternoon with her cousin would surely distract her from wayward urges.

"Taking a nap," Grammie answered, stirring her

stew once again. "I think I'm going to join her. I'm right tired this afternoon."

"Go ahead, Grammie," Millie urged. "I'll watch the food."

"That stew is fine. Don't mess with it. It just needs to simmer for a while."

Grammie liked full control of the cooking, and Millie knew better than to mess with Grammie's food. That might mean they'd all be eating burnt stew tonight, however. She took Grammie by the arm and led her to her tent, from which came a loud cacophony of snoring. Millie placed a kiss on Grammie's cheek, then ushered her inside, closing the tent flap behind her. She turned and faced the camp. Ben tended the horses, brushing them down, checking their feet. As was his way, he immersed himself totally in his task, oblivious to his surroundings.

Millie considered the man before her. She'd known him most of her life. He was a good sort and handsome enough to send most of the girls into a tither. So why had she never contemplated him as a man, as she recognized Raine as a man?

She found Ben to be extremely simple. True, he was handsome and sweet, but intellectually, she found him unstimulating. She considered him a big brother.

Looking again at the path Raine had taken into the woods, Millie moved to follow him. She didn't know why she followed, but her feet seemed to take her toward him with little regard for reason. She found him by a secluded pooling of water in the river. The deep area made a nice swimming spot. The late afternoon sun reflected on the water, creating a lazy, peaceful scene. She sensed his presence, though she hadn't seen him yet.

It was just the kind of place she would find pleasure in discovering, and without understanding why, assumed he would like the spot as well. She also spied his discarded clothes lying across a rock by the pool.

She should turn and go back to camp. She should, but she couldn't. Curiosity burned in her. She'd never seen a naked man before, and the notion of seeing this naked man drove her beyond good judgment. Sneaking closer, but still staying a safe distance away, she hid behind a bush. Fear of being discovered pounded in her veins, and then he surfaced, expelling a large gust of air.

A small sound escaped her as she watched his marvelous form swimming across the small pool, creating sensations inside her she'd never suffered before. The motion of his sleek, powerful body hypnotized her. She watched him splash, his bronzed body, hard, muscled, and magnificent. The blood in her temples throbbed as her heart beat wildly in her chest. The sight of him disturbed her in a strange, pleasurable sort of way, beyond what she could ever have imagined.

He didn't swim for long, and much to her alarm, he exited the water. As he dried himself, blood pounded in parts of her belly which had never stirred before. Unconsciously, she moved forward, realizing her mistake as a stick snapped beneath her weight. Much to her relief, Raine seemed not to have heard her as he continued drying himself. Realizing there was little time for gawking, she turned to escape. She began to crawl away quietly through the brush on her hands and knees but froze when footsteps pounded behind her.

"Well, well, well," he mocked.

She turned her head, his naked legs and feet immediately in sight. Her eyes rounded to near the size of a blue harvest moon, and she snapped her head back, eyes to the front, mortified at being this close to him in his current state of undress. Caught! Good God, she'd been caught! The hope that his heart would suddenly fail him was dwindling, and she feared she would not get out of this with her dignity intact.

"I suppose I should be flattered that you're spying on me."

Millie stood facing away from him. "Don't bother. I didn't even know you were there until it was too late. I didn't see anything." She displayed as much bravado as she could muster.

"That's a lie. I can tell by your color, which is quite amazing, by the way. You took a good long look. Or am I mistaken? Maybe this shade of…pink…is natural for you. And maybe you always crawl through the woods on your knees?"

There was nothing she could say that would save her from this humiliation. Her guilt was obvious.

He laughed, his amusement at her embarrassment greater than he could contain. "Turn around. You're already caught. You might as well get an eyeful to squelch your curiosity once and for all."

Millie shrieked, something she'd never done in her entire life, and took off in a dead run. As fast as an arrow out of the bow, she ran through the woods, his laughter close on her heels.

She ran without stopping, hoping she would have the stamina to run the hundreds of miles back to Kansas. The exertion helped cool her soul-searing humiliation. She slowed somewhat, satisfied she had put a safe distance between them. What had she been thinking? And how could she ever face him again? She would simply have to act as if nothing had happened, ignore him, including forgoing her sneak peeks at him. She would pray night and day they would reach her father's ranch soon. And she would definitely sleep in the tent from now on.

Still, she didn't think she could temper her desire for him, despite the fact he repeatedly made her feel like a fool. She'd never met a man who affected her so, creating such a deep and foreign ache within her. She could endure the embarrassment of confrontation with him, in exchange for the opportunity to figure out the turmoil of emotions his nearness caused.

Millie walked back toward camp, tears just at the brink of spilling down her cheeks, as she cursed her confusion where Raine was concerned. Suddenly, gunshots from camp reverberated through the air. Millie gulped down a lump of fear and took off toward the sound of the shots, terror replacing any shame she suffered. She ran as fast as her considerably long legs would carry her, when Raine passed her at an even faster pace.

She caught up with him in camp, as he stood outside of Grammie's tent, holding the flap open and looking inside. To Millie's relief, Grammie's voice rose above all the others. Millie followed Raine into the tent. He bent over the lifeless body of a man, and his expression displayed only mild irritation as he looked up at the old woman.

His voice, however, revealed his true level of exasperation. "Who the hell is this, and what the hell happened?"

"That no 'count cow puncher is Elias Wright. He worked for us at one time, but I fired him for stealing,"

Grammie told him.

Raine looked at Millie, letting his irritation show. This whole trip really had spiraled out of hand. "What's he doing here?" he asked Grammie.

"He tried to kill me." Grammie's face blazed with excitement and her voice contained no small amount of enthusiasm.

Chapter Eight

"Why?" Raine looked around the tent at the whiff of whiskey invading his nostrils to sniff out the source. He spotted the bottle beside Grammie's bunk. He picked it up, looked at it and then at Grammie, a considerable frown distorting his usually calm visage.

He tossed the bottle to Ben before turning away from the three of them, trying to get a grip on his composure. He massaged his temples, wanting to laugh despite the seriousness of the situation. It was all too much. He didn't need this crazy old lady getting drunk and shooting her hired help. He stared silently at the floor for a moment, then turned back to the four looking expectantly at him. Knowing when he was outnumbered, he surrendered. "What am I missing?" he asked.

"Someone wants to kill her." Millie told him.

Raine resisted the "besides me" comment, which sat on the edge of his tongue. He didn't think anyone would appreciate his levity.

"Who?" he asked instead.

This time Millie kept silent, but Ben did not. "Millie's beau."

Millie flinched, and immediately defended herself. "He's not my 'beau'."

"Can I dare to hope that he," Raine pointed to the short, fat, bald, and smelly Elias, "was your beau?"

Millie put her hands in her pockets and looked at

Raine defiantly. "I don't have a beau, and no, that's not who they are referring to."

"Why does your fiancé want your grandmother dead?"

Millie stamped her foot in frustration. "He's not my fiancé. He was Grammie's lawyer. She received an anonymous note, threatening her. We aren't sure if he sent it, but we think he most likely did. No one else would even dare sending such a thing."

Raine's anger simmered. "No one bothered to tell me any of this? I am responsible for your safety, all of your safety. Don't you think this bit of information might have been helpful in my protecting you?"

"We believed that by leaving, it was over. I never imagined anyone would follow us," Millie explained.

"Frankly, I didn't either," Ben supplied.

"What did the note say? Why did he threaten to kill her?"

"Money, of course." It was the first time Bridget had spoken in days.

Raine took stock of what he knew of Millie. Was she the sort to be involved in something like this? He'd had the feeling from the beginning she was hiding something. Maybe she'd been down at the river to make sure he stayed away, while this Elias did the job on the grandmother. It made sense, but he just couldn't convince himself she was anything but the curious innocent she seemed to be. But then again, women were masters at the art of deception. He'd have to keep a close eye on her. He couldn't afford to make a mistake, especially if Bridget's life might be in danger, along with her grandmother's. It would only make sense she may need to be eliminated as well, for Millie and her boyfriend to get any money.

"How do I know you're not in on any of this?" he asked Millie. He missed the withering look Ben and Margaret turned on him, since his attention fell fully upon her.

Aware of his scrutiny, she answered unwaveringly. "You don't."

That response struck a chord in Raine's mind. His accusation hadn't set her on the defensive. She didn't protest her innocence. If she'd been guilty, she most certainly would have. Still, he would leave no possibility out.

He turned his full attention to Margaret. "Do you have anything to add?"

"Parker Reynolds is a fool. He's stupid, and he's greedy." She spat tobacco juice into the middle of the group.

Ignoring that, or trying to, he continued his inquiry. "Do you think she could be in on this?" he asked, indicating Mille.

"Of course not," Grammie snapped, but she continued in a new, even tone. "Parker Reynolds moved to town and immediately solicited my legal business. I imagine he planned to rearrange my legal affairs without my knowing it. He courted Millie, but smart girl that she is, she rejected him, and then I found myself a new lawyer. He probably would have tried courting Bridget next but decided just to go for blood instead."

He digested Margaret's information. "Do you think you can refrain from shooting anyone else?"

She shrugged and turned her back on Raine, who scowled down at the dead body at his feet. He turned to Ben. "Come on. Let's get rid of this guy."

Another hour passed before Raine and Ben rejoined the three women by the fire. Grammie dozed lightly, the exhaustion of the day overtaking her. Ben, who'd been outside of camp gathering firewood on a skid at the time of the shooting, asked Bridget to recount the events which led up to the shooting death of their former hired hand, and everyone turned their attention to her story. She surmised Elias had snuck into their tent after she'd left it and had tried to murder Grammie. She'd heard nothing up until the sound of the same gunshot alerting everyone else. For a time, Raine held Millie under scrutiny.

****

She pretended not to notice, but as his stare intensified, she grew uneasy. When she turned her attention to him, he spoke softly to her, not wanting to awaken her grandmother. "This lawyer, Reynolds— neither of you would necessarily have to marry him. He could have false papers drawn up saying you were married, signed by a minister or a judge. There are people who can be paid to do anything. Does he have your signatures on anything?"

She let go of her defenses for once and sighed. "Yes, he would have mine. I handle most of the business for the ranch."

"That may have been the reason he pursued you, and not Bridget, something as simple as that. With your grandmother out of the way, it would be your word against his. If he has the legal documentation, he could discredit you. There are stories of men having their wives committed to insane asylums so they could inherit and control their fortunes." At her look of horror, he assured her, "It's heinous, I know, but some people are just that greedy—or desperate."

The crackling of the fire broke the silence falling upon the group. When Bridget and Grammie made their excuses for retiring, Ben decided that he, too, should retire for the night. Raine nodded and hauled Millie up by her elbow. The heat of his touch would remain long after he removed his hand.

"I think you all should turn in. I'm going to stay up, in case there are any others who decide to sneak into our camp and put their lives in your grandmother's hands."

Millie conceded. Knowing he would be looking out for their welfare made her feel considerably safer. She couldn't explain her turmoil of emotions regarding Raine, but he did make her feel safe. His obvious competence reassured her that she could trust him to protect them.

Raine walked Millie and her bedroll to Grammie's tent. When they reached the entrance, he stopped. "What? No argument?"

She shook her head. She had little fight left in her.

As the sun descended, Raine appeared to consider the camp. He appeared to be so deep in contemplation, it startled Millie when he opened his mouth to speak.

"Ever considered really getting married?"

His words stunned her momentarily. "Married?" Confusion marred her features. "Who would I marry? And why?"

"Well, how about Ben? You two seem close. Your boyfriend couldn't get the money if your marriage is registered legally in a courthouse somewhere, with witnesses. And he would no longer have reason to hurt your grandmother."

"That has some merit, I have to admit. But I can't

marry Ben. He's the type who would want to stay married."

"What's wrong with that? He's a decent fellow."

"He's great, but he's like a brother to me. I could never...well, I wouldn't want to...you know." It was clear he understood from the expectant grin on his face. She'd like to slap it off him. Then another idea came to her, and she smiled. That smile should have sent him running, but it captivated him completely, and he couldn't move.

"What if *you* married me?"

A parade of emotions crossed his face, but he regained his composure and matched her smile. "That's clever, but sorry, it's impossible."

"Why? Are you already married?"

"No. And I have no intention of ever getting married."

"Well then, we might as well forget about my getting married."

"Why? You just said it was a good idea."

"Yes." Millie agreed. She acquiesced instantly, so it was as if someone had slapped him when she continued, "but if you won't marry me, I won't marry anyone."

She turned on her heel and walked into Grammie's tent, leaving Raine speechless yet again.

Seeing that all evidence of Elias had been removed, she plopped herself down on her bedroll. If she'd had the time or the energy to cry, she would have, but exhausted both mentally and physically, she fell asleep as soon as she closed her eyes.

Chapter Nine

Millie had not wanted or expected to ride with Raine this morning. However, after yesterday's events, Raine ordered Ben to drive Grammie and Bridget's wagon with them secured in the back. Raine had obviously deemed her the lesser of the three evils and had assigned himself Millie duty. They'd ridden most of the day in silence, speaking only when necessary, her exceeding embarrassment by the events of the previous day curbing her desire to engage him.

Eastern Colorado was easy land to travel, flat land which allowed their horses to move fast and graze leisurely. Because Raine worried someone might follow them, he'd wasted no time in getting through the territory. Millie regarded her surroundings. Except for some slight blue bumps along the distant horizon, the landscape differed little from Kansas.

"What are you looking at?" Millie snapped, as she caught his regard. The silence between them wore on her nerves.

Raine's brows drew together, and he grunted, looking away.

Millie stuck out her tongue at his back and then looked at the retreating horizon. Shielding her eyes against the sun, she scanned the sky ahead for what seemed to be storm clouds looming in front of them. She looked at Raine, but he looked at the skyline with nothing other than an expression of boredom. Feeling her scrutiny, he looked back at her, but Millie looked away, turning her attention back over the land.

She became bored by the endlessness of flat land, and her imagination began to run away with her. She could envision an attack by hostiles. *They would capture her and Raine. Her glowing auburn hair would awe the Natives. Thinking her a daughter of the sun god, they would release her. It would be up to her to save Raine. Should she risk it?*

He is awfully pretty. She studied him. And the loss of that silky black scalp would certainly be a shame. She turned to look behind her. She would have the others to think about if captured, and rescuing Raine might just bring the hostiles' wrath down on her friends and family. Could she sacrifice Raine's perfect hairline for the sake of the others? No, if she but looked into those pleading, sapphire blue orbs, she would never be able to leave him to suffer at the mercy of the savages.

She would wait until dark, when the Indians were sleeping peacefully, and she would sneak into their camp. Finding Raine tied and gagged behind the Chief Great Bear's teepee, his spirit beaten and his will exhausted, she would quietly free him. The gratitude and adoration would be obvious in his eyes. She'd pat him on the shoulder comfortingly, then with a finger to her lips to quiet any words of gratitude he might be compelled to speak, she'd place her arm around his waist so he could put his weight on her, as he'd be too weak to walk to her horse alone. As they rode off, several braves would make to follow, but Millie would hold them off with gunfire, injuring no one. They would escape to a nearby cave, and hold up there for the night, until the furor of the escape died down. His new feelings for her would be raw. "I love you, Mildred," he would say. "You are the bravest, the most beautiful..."

"What are you grinning about?" Raine asked, abruptly interrupting her private melodrama.

Millie instantly dropped her smile. "I was fantasizing about a slow, torturous death for you."

"Tsk. Tsk. And to think just last night you wanted to marry me. Are you always so fickle?

Millie shrugged. "Hey. It was your idea. I just wanted to see if you were at all as heroic as you try to portray yourself. Obviously not."

He tried to absolve himself. "Look, I'm sorry, but Ben is a much better candidate than I am. You're entirely too young for me," he told her, faltering.

Her posture straightened. "I'm almost twenty. You'll have to do better than that. We're talking about a rescue here, not a real marriage."

"You have red hair, for another thing." She missed his smile indicating the tease in his words.

"Well, you have an enormous nose," she threw at him.

"I do not!" He bellowed his own defense.

Millie turned away to hide her smile but couldn't suppress the laughter which came bubbling up.

Clearly exasperated, Raine closed his eyes and shook his head, chuckling softly. "Why don't you tell me why you won't consider Ben as a husband?"

She looked at him, then looked away, hating to fuel his ego any further. "I wouldn't feel right putting him in danger. Being my husband might prove deadly."

"But you wouldn't mind putting me in danger. That's where the slow and torturous death comes in, no doubt."

Millie shook her head. "It's not that. I just feel you could protect yourself, whereas I don't think Ben has ever been in a fight in his life. He's not exactly worldly. I'd hate to see him get hurt because of me."

Raine sat without saying a word, his silence urging her to continue.

"Besides," eyes downcast, she broke the silence. "I know you wouldn't want to stay married. Like I said, I think Ben would take his role of husband to heart, and I'm not ready. The idea of...with Ben...turns my stomach. He's like my brother."

"I don't think he thinks of you as his sister."

Millie nodded, then, without warning, she stopped. Raine stopped too and followed her gaze. The clouds ahead were breaking and rising. A wall of mountains rose up in the midst of them, which was unlike anything Millie could have imagined. She looked at Raine, and he smiled proudly as he continued to look forward.

"The Rocky Mountains."

****

As Millie stared in awe at the snow-covered, jagged peaks of the purple mountains, Raine turned and studied her.

"I've never imagined anything so magnificent. They fill the sky!" Millie kicked her horse forward. Raine smiled and kicked his horse, too. He followed her gaze again, back over the prairie to the mountains now discernible ahead. He experienced a certain amount of satisfaction at her reaction to the scene. He turned and watched her.

He, too, recognized the sting of their increasingly impossible relationship. His desire for her warred not only with his own conscience but also with her impossible naïveté. And her innocence conflicted with her damnable curiosity. All of which fueled her appeal and threatened to lead him to an unbearable situation.

The intermittent sun, when it shone through the clouds, highlighted her hair, making it glow as if on fire. Her perfect profile, with her high cheekbones, small straight nose, and full sensuous lips, beat any he had seen on even the most classically beautiful women he'd known. Millie had something earthy about her which beckoned him, something so natural in her beauty, he found himself drawn to her despite her hellcat's disposition.

And she'd asked him to marry her. The offer tempted him, only because of his eagerness to get his hands on her. He understood her argument about the difficulty of getting an annulment from Ben. He was certain, too, if Ben found himself married to Millie, it would be hard to convince him to give her up.

She obviously reasoned he disliked her so much she wouldn't have any trouble getting rid of him. If she only understood how he'd fought with himself to stay away from her. And having spent some time around her, he had to admit he admired her spirit. He'd never met a woman like her. Getting to know her fueled his desire for her.

The idea was absurd, so why had he been batting it around in his head since last night, as if it were a possibility? Well, for one, her life might be in danger, and he didn't like having that on his conscience.

"When I first met your grandmother, she offered me a probable fortune to marry her granddaughter. I assumed at the time she meant Bridget." He cocked his head as he continued. "But maybe she meant for me to marry you, to get the two of you out of this mess."

Millie gave him a lopsided smile. "I'd say she was testing you. What did you say?"

"That I couldn't be bought."

"Then you passed." She looked back at the mountains. "She wanted to see what kind of man you are. To be honest, I doubt she was offering either of us, but I suspect if you'd accepted, she'd have married you to Bridge, just to keep her out of trouble."

Raine shuddered. "It would be no less than a man deserved for selling off the rest of his life."

"She's not that bad." Millie clearly had a habit of defending her cousin.

"That's what I keep telling myself."

Millie regarded him closely.

"How are you two related to each other?" he asked her.

She kept her reply casual. "I don't know that we are."

"Well, that doesn't make any sense. Is she your cousin, or isn't she?"

"I honestly don't know. Grammie adopted Bridget when she was very young. We've grown up together and just always called each other cousin. And Grammie has always been Grammie to both of us."

Raine considered her answer for a moment. "I think the whole lot of you are insane, if you want my opinion," he assured her with a look of mock disapproval.

"I'm surprised you noticed." Her smile was genuine. "Most people are so confused when they're around all three of us at once, they walk away feeling a little addled themselves."

Raine laughed and their eyes met. With the

animosity between them temporarily gone, an intense current flowed between them. She looked away.

Raine cleared his throat. "What do you say we take tomorrow off? We can camp at the foot of those mountains and rest up for a day before we have to do any climbing."

"We're going to climb those mountains?" Millie asked in disbelief.

"We'll have to cross them. There's a pass up ahead, and that will be quicker than going to Casper, then down again. We'll be in Wyoming soon, and only a few days of hard traveling to Laramie. From there, it will be a fairly easy ride to the ranch."

"What do you mean by 'hard traveling'?"

Raine's laughter floated behind him as he kicked his horse and rode ahead.

Chapter Ten

Once camp had been set up, a tranquil feeling settled in on Millie. The temporary truce with Raine eased her mind. She'd enjoyed their easy conversation today. She enjoyed just being around him, even when they argued, to a certain extent. She enjoyed sparring with him, his masculinity adding a certain aspect of stimulation to the argument she'd found with neither Bridget nor Grammie.

Things had certainly turned around today. Now she found when she caught his eye, a smile would light his handsome face, instead of that disheartening frown. A certain amount of pleasure flooded her, and she smiled back, despite her desire to remain aloof. The man could be charming when he applied himself.

The horizon glowed with red and orange streaks. Above that the sky turned into a deep purple sea of tranquility. Having eaten a better than usual meal from Grammie, she leaned back on a log. Crossing her arms under her head, she watched the stars materialize from the depths of the darkening cloak above.

She listened as Ben began crooning "Texas Rangers" somewhere in the dark behind her. Unable to lie still and relax because of the churning of her emotions, she sat up and looked around. She didn't see Raine anywhere. What reason could he have to disappear into the darkness other than to avoid her? Did he think her a complete fool, declaring she'd marry him and no one else? Could he possibly know how much she wanted him, wanted all of him, marriage or not? Groaning loudly in frustration, she collapsed backward again and threw her arms across her face, as if that would erase her distress.

She sighed. It would be the last time. Maybe Grammie would still be awake to keep her company. Hoisting herself up, she walked toward the dim light burning within Grammie's tent. Pushing back the flap, she poked her head in and found Grammie relaxing on her makeshift cot with a whiskey in hand.

"Hi, Grammie. Are you feeling well?"

"I'm fine, darlin'. Come on in here and sit with me a spell."

"Where's Bridge?"

"I suspect she's down by the creek. Raine is with her."

Millie didn't hide her surprise. "Raine? How did she manage that?"

Grammie laughed. "Good question. I think she wants to practice her charm a bit before she gets to Denver. He went grudgingly, I assure you." She leaned forward conspiratorially. "I think he's a little afraid of her, truth be known." She chuckled at her joke.

Millie smiled wanly. She tried not to let her disappointment show, but her grandmother knew her all too well. Clucking her tongue, she looked at her granddaughter with a half-cocked smile.

"Why don't we tell him who you really are, honey? We will have to soon, either way."

Millie bit her fingernail, but refrained, balling her hand into a fist and resting it in her lap. She sighed heavily. "Most people are so superficial with me. So many of them don't approve of me, the way I've worked and lived, but they won't let on. They'll talk about me as if I were some sort of scandal when I'm not around, but to my face, they'll grease me up like they were going to slip me in a biscuit and eat me, just because I'll inherit your ranch someday. Well, would have…" She gave Grammie a pointed glare. "The money, in their eyes, made me somebody. I won't be any more important when you're gone than I am now, probably even less so."

Grammie's sympathetic smile urged her on.

"I noticed how he pampered Bridget, and I enjoyed being someone other than a girl with a big inheritance for a change. He thinks I'm nobody, which I am. I like it that way. I can face him on my own terms, and it feels good."

"Do you have feelings for him?" Grammie asked.

Millie didn't even blink at the question. "I honestly don't know."

Grammie didn't respond but looked down her nose through her spectacles at her, waiting.

Millie put her chin in her hands and rested her elbows on her knees and sighed heavily. "I asked him to marry me, you know."

"That's my girl, Millie. Go after what you want…"

"No. It wasn't like that. He had the idea I marry, to throw Parker off track."

Grammie nodded her approval at that line of reasoning. Millie gave her a look of dismay.

"I told him I'd marry him or no one." She cast her forlorn expression to the floor. "I'll tell him soon. This ridiculous masquerade has gone on long enough. It isn't fair to him. I imagine he'll be mad as a hornet when he finds out."

"Maybe he'll be relieved."

"How so?"

"You and he seem to get along well enough, whereas he cringes every time he looks at Bridget. Seeing as how your father's daughter will live with them, seems he might be pleased if she were someone agreeable."

"He seems to find Bridget agreeable enough. Otherwise, would he be out strolling through the moonlight with her?"

"Jealousy doesn't become you, darlin'. I'm sure the boy feels a certain obligation toward Bridget. I'm not unaware of his relationship with your father. Raine isn't your pa's natural son, but your pa adopted him many years ago. Raine believes he owes your father for his life. It's only his duty to treat Tom's 'daughter' with care and civility, no matter how distasteful the task."

"Grammie, you shouldn't talk about Bridget that way. After all, you've raised her for many years. I can't believe you don't harbor deep affection for her."

"Millie, I've tried. But the girl is the most hateful, ungrateful little polecat."

"Yes, I know she doesn't treat you right. She doesn't understand where she'd be without you."

"That girl thinks the world owes her whatever she wants. She has no idea of value or worth, because everything has always been handed to her. That's my fault, I guess, but even as a babe, she expected things, and it was easier to give it to her than to listen to her tirades. You never expected anything from anybody, and I'll be damned if you didn't get mad if anyone tried to give you anything."

"Well, I get bored if things are too easy," Millie

smiled. Grammie covered Millie's hand with her own.

"It's all about how you treat folks. You have to treat them with some decency, no matter who they are. If there was one thing I tried to teach you girls, it was that. With Bridge, it just didn't sink in. She treats everyone the same, granted, but that treatment is that they're a mat for her to wipe her boots on."

"She's still young, Grammie. She'll mature yet. You'll see. Don't give up on her."

"I won't give up on her, honey. But don't expect too much from her. Some are just evil seed. I know about these things."

Millie had the feeling Grammie wanted to say more, but the old woman kept her silence. When the time was right, Grammie would tell her what she held back now. Grammie seemed to have a precise sense of timing, and Millie had learned to trust that.

Chapter Eleven

Raine spent most of the morning debating with himself whether he should even approach Bridget and attempt, once again, to carry on a conversation with her. After all, the woman would live on the ranch with them. He needed to be civil, at least. And damned if he hadn't tried. But every time he made the effort, she complained and railed at him. Or worse, she pouted cunningly, expecting him to talk about her pretty dress, or how she wore her hair.

Then there was Millie. Today, of all days, he should avoid her like a cottonwood with a noose swinging from it. She'd gotten to him yesterday, and he'd lain awake, actually considering marrying her, just to help her out, he told himself. When he finally did go to sleep, he'd almost convinced himself to go through with it. But luckily, in the chill of the early morning, his senses had returned.

He'd been haunted his entire life by a father who felt trapped by his obligations to his family. His father was a mountain man, a wanderer, never at ease in one place. Then he'd fallen in love with a Cheyenne maiden and had tried to make a life with his new family. He couldn't settle, however. He left, with a promise to return, but then the soldiers came to Sand Creek. Raine's mother was killed, along with many of his tribe. Raine survived. His father was never seen again, and Raine never knew what happened to him. Raine swore never to put himself in the position of having that responsibility, binding himself to someone who would look to him for protection, protection he may not be able to provide.

He spotted Bridget alone on a blanket by her wagon. She sewed a brightly colored patch of quilt, or at least attempted the procedure.

"Need some help with that?"

She raised her chin and looked down the short length of her nose at him. "Why would I need a man's help with sewing?" she asked, her tone biting.

"Well, for one thing, even I know you're supposed to use thread." He smiled at her, thinking she too would find humor in her oversight.

"Oooh! Where did you ever learn your manners? Listen, that backwoodsy charm may work on some people," she gave a pointing glare at Millie, sitting some distance away, "But I assure you, I prefer my men civilized." She returned a leveling gaze to Raine. "Let's try, shall we?"

"Are you serious?" Raine laughed, thinking she was being coy.

"Quite." She sniffed and brushed imaginary dust off her lap, dismissing him.

Raine gave a low whistle and shook his head. *Poor Tom.* Raine turned to look at Millie and smiled unwillingly. Most of the women he'd known in his life had been like Bridget. Millie, however, was a breath of cool air on a hot day. Even though she provoked him at every turn, she was refreshing, so amusing with her tomboy antics and her totally unpretentious manner. She made him feel good. It was as simple as that.

"Excuse me," he offered as an afterthought, leaving

Bridget and walking toward where Millie sat cross-legged under the tree, reading a book. He stood above her, his immense frame shadowing her small one. She looked up at him and smiled back.

"What?" she asked.

"Come on." He jerked his head toward the river. "Let's go fishing." He didn't give her a chance to refuse but grabbed her arm and hauled her up.

****

Her insides fluttered at his touch. She wouldn't have been able to refuse, regardless. He was helplessly charming in his current mood.

"Why the sudden interest in fish?" She struggled to keep up with the pace set by his long stride, her faithful dog trotting beside her.

"We can catch ourselves a fresh supper. Have any objections to that?"

"Sounds like a marvelous idea."

"You can fish, can't you?"

"I'm sure I can. Couldn't be too hard, after all, if you can do it."

He continued his steady pace ahead of her. Not wanting to question his playful mood, she followed him without protest.

They found the creek, which to Millie looked like a river. It was wide and shallow, and the water broke roughly on boulders scattered throughout. Aspen trees were thick along the bank, and as the wind hissed and rattled through the tear-shaped leaves, Millie believed the place surely must be magical.

Raine removed his hat, throwing it to the ground behind him. He broke off two branches and pulled some string and two small hooks from the leather bag in his pocket. He tied the string to the end of each branch and the small hooks to the ends of the string. Taking two crickets from the bag, he baited each hook. Handing Millie one of the newly made rods, he turned to the river and plopped himself on top of the short, steep bank. Dropping his line in at the edge of the water and anchoring his makeshift pole in the soft ground, he stretched himself, extending the length of his body into a reclining position on top of the short bank. Millie sat next to him on the damp ground, and copied his fishing technique of casting and anchoring, but decided against lying down beside him, even though the position looked invitingly comfortable. Jack found a nice place for a nap in the sunshine a few feet away.

"Well?" she asked.

His eyes were hooded, his arms behind his head, his ankles crossed casually. "Well, what?"

"What do we do now?"

He opened one eye and smiled wickedly, for which he received an uncertain frown. Turning his attention to the blue sky, he shrugged in answer. "We wait for the fish, of course."

"How long do we wait?"

"As long as it takes."

She laughed this time, convinced he didn't care if he caught a fish. He was loafing. She was flattered he wanted to loaf with her. She looked around at the beautiful day. It was certainly a day for nothing but enjoyment. She filled her lungs with dry, cool air and smiled as she exhaled. Yes, it was a perfect day for fishing. Without realizing it, she lay back next to Raine, folding her arms behind her head and looking up at the same brilliant sky which now held his attention. The sun warmed her skin, the cool air swirled about her face, and the combination of the sensations was heady. She closed her eyes, and her senses came alive in the autumn air. She relaxed, listening to the birds, the rushing water, the wind in the leaves, and then she concentrated on Raine's deep breathing. Her body flushed at his closeness. Her breathing soon took on the rhythm of his, and she became completely absorbed in the man lying beside her.

"What kind of name is 'Raine'?" Her eyebrows rose and she cocked her head to one side. "Indian?"

Raine looked at her, clearly surprised she had guessed his heritage. He regarded her closely. "Yes, as a matter of fact. Cheyenne." She didn't flinch. "Well, sort of," he clarified, as he looked back up at the sky. "That's not my actual name."

"What is your real name?"

Rolling onto his side and propping his elbow to support his head in his hand, he was silent for a moment before answering. His true name carried a great deal with it—memories, tragedy, prejudice—and he wondered if he could trust her with the weight of it. Regarding her profile with warmth in his narrowed eyes, his voice came out in a husky whisper. "Sleeping Storm."

She considered the name for some time and then surprised him again by saying aloud. "I like that. It suits you."

"How so?" he asked, smiling faintly.

"Your coloring, your eyes—stormy." She looked over at him. "Your temperament."

His laugh was rich, deep. "It didn't take Tom long to understand how I was named either. When we were first together, we came upon a group of soldiers. They baited Tom for being with me. I think they intended to kill me—as they'd just killed my family."

"What happened?"

"One of the soldiers put a gun to Tom's head and another held me with a knife to my scalp. At that moment, I understood that Tom was willing to die for me." He grunted softly, a faraway look in his eyes as he remembered.

"'Are you an injun lover?' I remember the soldier asking Tom." Raine lifted his hair to show her a scar still evident at his hairline. "The soldier made a deep gash. Then he moved the knife to my throat. There was a lot of blood running down my face. It was hard to see, but I looked at Tom. The soldier was going to kill me. I really didn't care at that point, and I refused to show fear. I think Tom believed I was half crazed."

"What happened?" Millie was breathless with anticipation, eager to hear the rest of the story.

Raine shrugged.

"Tell me! You can't end there."

"It's hard to remember clearly. Tom and I have never talked about it. But I bit into the soldier's forearm and took a chunk out of it. When he loosened his grip, I grabbed his hand and bent back all his fingers, and there were loud crackling pops. I'd broken them. He fell to his knees, dropping the knife. I grabbed it and tackled one of the other soldiers. I pressed the knife to his jugular. Tom took the gun from the one holding it on him, as he was a bit stunned by what was happening."

"And? What happened next?"

A grim line crossed his lips, and his eyes became shadowed. "I think I would have killed him, but Tom stopped me. I was so filled with hatred at what they'd done to my people, I couldn't see anything else. I remember what Tom said to me at the time. 'If you and I are going to make it in this world, we have to put these things behind us.' He said, 'I know you're hurting, but what you're thinking of doing will hurt you the rest of your life.' We left then, and he told me I would have to learn to live in this world, like it or not. He said I would find that there were people who didn't like what the soldiers had done to my family any more than he or I did. He told me about his wife's death and the loss of his daughter. I think we reached an understanding then."

"How did you come to be called 'Raine'?"

"Tom sought to whiten my name a little. The hands were always making fun of me when I was a boy. 'Angry all the time, steady as rain,' they'd say. It's practically legend around the ranch that I carried my own cloud around with me."

"How did you come to be with him?"

"Tom?" Raine lay back down beside her. "He bought me."

Her sharp intake of breath was gratifying. "What?" The concept appalled her.

"True enough. My family was…killed. I ended up with a friend of my father's. She sold me to Tom."

Millie sat up and faced him, hugging her knees to her chest. "Was your mother Indian?"

Raine nodded. "And my father was French, a trapper who had a hard time abandoning his way of life. He spent most of his time in the Tetons, but died there, I suppose. We never saw him again."

"You're not bitter?"

"What's the point? He couldn't stay in one place for long, and he couldn't very well have toted his family along with him. He assumed we'd be safe with my mother's people. He'd leave and come back every year. But when he didn't return, I knew something had happened to him. Despite his restlessness, he really loved my mother very much. Eventually, I grew to care for Tom as much as I did my actual parents. I've had a good life, and I suppose Tom was glad to have me, since he lost his wife and daughter."

"And now, you are taking his daughter to him." She spoke mostly to herself. And then to Raine, "How does he feel about her coming?"

"Scared, I think." Raine sat up, silent for a moment. "I think he always hoped his daughter and I would marry." Raine picked up a broken twig and began dissecting it.

"It would be convenient for you, I think. Marriage, I mean. It would make sense for you to marry Thomas McConnell's daughter. You'd be like family, living there together." Millie's words made little sense, even in her own mind. But pieces of ideas were coming together somewhere in her brain, jumbled and ill-fitted because of the deception, in which she herself was a participant. She found herself jealous of the relationship Raine and Bridget might have, if Bridget were indeed Thomas' daughter. She wanted verification that he had no interest in Bridget.

Raine shook his head. "I promised myself I wouldn't involve myself with her."

"Why not?"

"I owe him too much. I can't take any more from him. And the responsibility I would feel to keep her happy, especially if we didn't suit each other, which we wouldn't, would be an impossible obligation to fill. And obviously, Bridget needs more than I'd be able to give."

His mocking tone and somewhat twisted smile betrayed his amusement.

Suddenly, anger filled her at getting so entangled in her deception. How could she win a war when the battle lines were so muddled by untruths? She didn't even know how to respond to his idiotic theories for fear of giving herself away.

"What if you had fallen in love with her?"

Raine shook his head again. "No."

"You'd sacrifice your happiness for him?"

"Something like that."

"Do you have someone? I mean…" Millie stammered at the awkwardness of her line of questioning. Still, she wanted to know badly enough to pursue it. "Are you in love with anyone now? Do you ever plan to marry?"

He shook his head and sighed. "I don't meet a lot of women, and the ones I know serve only one purpose for a man."

Millie blushed. She understood exactly to what kind of women he referred, and she couldn't help the jealousy which swelled within her. She rose to leave before he could witness her expression, which must surely be marked with her growing frustration.

He stopped her, however, grabbing her arm and pulling her back down beside him. She looked away, embarrassed by her childish behavior.

Raine smiled and lay back down to stare at the sky. "Anyway, Bridget's not exactly what I had hoped she'd be, for Tom's sake, that is."

"And what did you hope she'd be?"

Folding his hands back behind his head, he narrowed his eyes at the sky. "Someone more like you."

His words, as quiet as they were, hit her with the force of thunder. While she digested the meaning of his words, he spoke casually. "You have a bite."

She looked at him, confusion marking her brow. With an amused grin, he looked over his boots at her twitching pole. "On your line…a fish."

"Oh!" she exclaimed. Glad for the distraction, she easily rolled to her feet to fetch her rod. Getting her footing in the soft mud on the water's edge was difficult, because of the bank's steep incline, but as soon as her heels were dug in sufficiently, she reached down and picked up her pole. The weight of the fish pulled on the other end of the fragile line, and she pulled steadily on her end. Raine stood close behind her, breaking her concentration.

"Help me!" she yelled, laughing at the absurdity of what she attempted to do with the doomed fishing rod. He wrapped his arms around her and grabbed her hands on the pole. Unexpected as that was, she didn't complain, delighted, and a little shocked, at the feel of his body pressed against hers. The heat that ran the length of her made it difficult to concentrate on the task at hand. A shudder ran through her, but she fought to ignore it.

She pulled on her pole and once again the fish pulled in the opposite direction, strong and steady this time. She yanked hard, snapping the line, and squarely hitting Raine in the face with the snapped rod. With the pull gone on the other end, she lost her balance and almost fell backward.

She righted herself immediately, only succeeding in leaning too far forward. Her flailing form threatened to fall headfirst into the shallow water. Raine grabbed her hips, trying to balance her, but when her backside bumped his groin, he bent at the waist, sending them both into the stream with a splash. Jack stood on the edge of the water and barked. Millie surfaced first, letting out a shrill scream at the frigid water. Raine rolled over, laughing, and when Millie tried to get out, he pulled her back down, forcing another scream out of her.

Raine stood, picking her up in his arms, and trudged out of the thigh-deep water up onto the top of the bank. Feet firmly planted on the ground, he dropped Millie's legs and let her body slide down deliberately along his. Millie believed for sure he would kiss her, and she turned her face up expectantly when suddenly, an unknown force spun Raine around.

Raine's head swiveled with the stunning impact of a fist on his jaw, and he shook his head to clear his vision. He secured a punch on a man he'd barely even seen, and Millie shouted, "Stop!"

The stranger immediately halted any motion and looked at Millie, but Raine cautiously kept his eyes on the burly ape. The dangerous glint in his eye made Raine wary.

"Raine, this is John Reichman," Millie offered, looking to each of them to make certain they had calmed.

Raine raised a sarcastic eyebrow toward the scruffy giant. "A friend of yours?" He tested his bruised jaw.

"He's, uh," Millie stammered, "he's a private detective I hired."

Raine gave a caustic grunt. "I supposed he might be your fiancé."

Millie wanted to shriek at him that Parker Reynolds was not her fiancée but decided not to waste her breath. John Reichman snorted, obviously humored at the idea of him being her betrothed.

The two men eyed one another, each man estimating the other. John Reichman conceded first.

"Sorry about the intrusion." He indicated the spot where he had landed his fist on Raine's jaw. "I heard a scream, and I assumed…"

Raine rubbed his jaw. "No problem. I'm getting used to things getting a little strange when I'm around her."

The brawny man picked up his hat and dusted it off. Placing it on his matted head, he chuckled. Raine seemed to like the man's easy humor immediately. It vexed Millie that they joked so casually at her expense.

John Reichman extended his hand to Raine. "They call me 'Beauty'," he told him.

Raine extended his dripping arm to shake his hand and replied, "I can't imagine why," bringing another heavy snort of laughter from the man. "They call me Raine." The two nodded in greeting, and Raine continued, "You must be here for a reason. My guess would be it has something to do with Parker Reynolds?"

Beauty nodded. "He's in the area, and he's heading North, apparently on the same trail, about fifty miles in front of you."

Millie looked at Raine to judge his reaction to the news.

"Do you think he knows where we're going?" Millie asked.

Beauty nodded.

Raine frowned at that. "There are a lot of places to hide in these parts, and places where he could lie in wait for us. If he knows where we're going, he will be plotting against either you or your grandmother."

"You mean you won't be able to protect her?" Millie

asked Raine.

"He may know the territory, darlin', but he doesn't know it as well as I do. I know places Reynolds couldn't find with a map." Grinning, he pulled his hat down on his forehead, making an exaggerated show of tipping it to her. She smiled at the gesture but took a slow, deep breath, trying to loosen the tightening in her chest. She was concerned not only for Grammie's safety, but now also surprisingly, for Raine's.

Chapter Twelve

The rustling of canvas woke Millie, and she reached for the gun stashed under her pillow. She cocked it and pointed it at the tent opening, intending to shoot, until the sound of her name came to her across the darkness. She experienced a measure of relief at Bridget's voice, but some amount of irritation at having been awoken when it had taken her most of the night to fall asleep. Millie waved the gun in the darkness, still contemplating shooting, then fell back on her pillow and released the hammer to remove any temptation. Reaching behind her, she lit the lard oil lantern and gave Bridge a deep frown. Cold air filled the tent. Ben had watch over the camp for the night, so she slept in his tent to get away from Bridget's intolerable snoring. She pushed her unruly hair off her face.

"In or out, Bridge," she commanded.

"I'm comin' in. I can't sleep. All that barkin' gives me the creeps." Millie could sympathize with that. She'd lain awake for hours listening to the howl of the coyotes. Bridget entered the tent and sat on the edge of Millie's cot. She smoothed out her skirt, an odd gesture, Millie deemed, considering the time of night.

"How about some tea?" Bridge asked pleasantly, as if attending an afternoon luncheon.

Still dozy, Millie's voice crackled. "Tea? At this time of night?"

"Oh, just give me somethin' to drink, anything," she snapped. "What do you have?"

"This isn't exactly a luxury hotel I'm sleeping in," Millie told her. "I have water. And not awfully good water."

"Give me some." Impatiently, Bridge held out her hand.

With a grunt, Millie pushed herself off her bed and filled a cup for Bridge and one for herself. Not far off, a coyote yipped. Bridge jumped, but Millie stopped to listen. She liked to hear them, liked the wildness of it, even though their mournful sounds sometimes sent goose bumps down the length of her. She pictured Raine out there somewhere.

Bridge shook in an exaggerated shudder. "They sound so close. How far away do you think they are?" she asked.

Millie rolled her eyes. "I don't know." She lay back down on top of her narrow bed, trying to avoid Bridge's big bottom planted near the end.

"Look outside for me and see if there's anything out there."

Millie's irritation showed. Bridget had avoided her the entire trip. When Millie had gone to her in search of some companionship, Bridget had told her to go away and leave her alone. Now she had come to her tent in the middle of the night.

"Please, Millie," implored Bridget, sweetly this time.

"How did you walk over her if you're so scared?"

"I didn't want to be alone. Please look outside. Just make me feel better."

"Good grief." Millie got out of her bed and walked

over to the tent flap. Growling with frustration, she cast a frown over her shoulder and went outside. She made an exaggerated show of looking to the left, then to the right, and turned back inside, eager to be rid of Bridget and get back to her warm bed. She'd been having such a nice dream.

"See anything?"

"No."

"Good." Bridget swallowed her water in one gulp and put the cup back down. She folded her hands demurely in her lap and looked up expectantly at Mille. "Do you know where Grammie is?"

Millie sat on the edge of the bed and wrapped a blanket around herself. She picked up her cup and shrugged the blanket higher up on her shoulders. "No, I don't. Raine took her somewhere to hide her and keep her safe. He wouldn't tell me where." She lifted her tin cup to her lips and drank, frowning at the bitter taste left in her mouth. It was next to impossible to get a clean cup to drink out of on this trip, not to mention water that wasn't stale.

Bridget studied her closely. "I can't believe they wouldn't even tell you."

"Well, believe it. I do not know. Raine told me he'd be back before morning, so you can ask him."

"Hmmm. Well," Bridget muttered. "I'm going." She stretched halfheartedly, concealing a small yawn behind soft, delicate fingers. "I'm suddenly so tired." She reached for Millie's boots, and with a sneer, stuck her hand distastefully inside one of them. "I'm going to borrow this." She pulled Millie's single shot derringer out of the boot with two fingers and gave Millie a satisfied smirk. "Sweet dreams, Cuz."

Millie watched her leave as swiftly as she'd entered, rolling her eyes once again at her cousin's strange behavior. She didn't much like Bridget taking her pistol, but if it made her feel safer, let her have it. She still had her pistol. Yawning, she stood to shut out the night air behind Bridget. She picked up her revolver off her bed and placed it back under the pillow. Bridget acted bizarrely these days, beyond her usual.

Straightening, Millie blinked hard to refocus her eyes. Putting her hand to her head, she groaned inwardly, suddenly dreadfully disoriented. As she turned for the bed, she clumsily bumped the stand that held her water, loudly knocking it and its contents to the floor. As her vision blurred again, fear immediately gripped her. Frowning, she touched a hand to the canvas above her head to get her bearings in the reeling tent.

Instinctively, she comprehended her circumstances. She tried to remain standing, but regardless of her efforts, she fell to her knees. With all her remaining strength, she tried to shout, but only managed a whisper. "Bridget…" Reality rapidly slipped, and she tried once again to stand, but this time, she fell flat on the floor.

****

Raine circled camp, a mile directly west, instead of riding right into it. He didn't want to make it obvious to anyone who might note such a thing, from which direction he'd come. When he entered camp, things seemed too still, too quiet. Were they all still sleeping? And where was Ben, who was supposed to be on watch? A sickening feeling hit him. Something was wrong. He looked in Bridget's tent. Empty. Closing the distance to the last tent with long stomping strides, he practically pulled the tent down upon entering. No one. The camp

106

was ominously quiet.

Breaking through the silence, however, came a groan from Ben, a short distance from his tent. Kneeling down on one knee, Raine supported him as he tried to rise to a sitting position.

"I tried to stop them," Ben told him.

Raine swore under his breath. How could he have been such a fool? He'd played right into Millie's hands. He'd acted like a fool. He looked at Ben, feeling guilty for wanting to pulverize him, and knowing at the same time, the blame didn't belong on him.

"It's my fault." Raine squeezed Ben's shoulder reassuringly, furious with himself for not making sure Bridget had been better protected. "Without the old woman, they won't kill Bridget. I'll get her back."

Ben looked at Raine and frowned. "You don't understand."

"What don't I understand?"

"Millie's in danger."

"Well, they're both gone, and I'll get them both back." Ben nodded and Raine ran his fingers through his hair. He frowned, unable to justify the spiraling apprehension within him.

Raine looked to Ben. "Can you make it back on your own?"

Ben shook his head. "I'm going with you."

"No, partner. That bump on your head is serious. I want you to rest here a couple of days. There's plenty of food and firewood. You'll be okay here." At Ben's obvious reluctance, he stated flatly, "I can move faster without you." Ben locked eyes with Raine and nodded.

An understanding passed between the two men, and Ben pleaded hoarsely, "Just find her."

"I will," Raine assured him. "I'll find them both."

Chapter Thirteen

Millie awoke before sunup, mainly because she was freezing. Her feet were bare, and she had no blanket. Her head threatened to split from the pounding inside it. Opening one eye carefully, afraid the effort might indeed tear her head open, she surveyed her surroundings, which, to her dismay, were totally unfamiliar. Looking around the cramped, filthy room and getting no clues as to her whereabouts, she closed her eyes again. Of course, Parker had done this. She tried to remember her last moments of consciousness, and suddenly the memory returned with crystal clarity.

"Bridget." Her voice came out a ragged whisper. She covered her eyes, the coolness of her hand easing the pain only a bit. How could she have been so unsuspecting of her? She should have been on guard, but she'd sorely misjudged her cousin. And she could have never dreamed Bridget would have the guile to drug and aid in a kidnapping. She didn't want to believe it. There must be some other explanation.

Raine had taken Grammie out of camp and stashed her somewhere safe, which gave her some solace. She wondered how Raine would react to her disappearance. He'd most likely be glad to be rid of her, since she'd been such a constant thorn in his side, and that idea made her want to cry. But she wouldn't, not now.

She massaged her throbbing temples when footsteps

outside caught her attention. Automatically, she reached for her pistol, but it wasn't there. Then she reached for the derringer she usually strapped to her leg but remembered she had taken it off before she'd climbed into bed.

She looked around the ramshackle cabin to the door as it opened, and there stood quite possibly the ugliest man she'd ever seen staring back at her with hollow, evil eyes. Seeing she was awake, he approached her watchfully, reminding Millie of a slithering snake in the cold of January. Wanting to have an advantage if an opportunity to flee presented itself, she stood.

A sickening dread filled her. "Who the hell are you?" she bit out, trying to hide the terror in her veins.

"Nobody." His tight, raspy voice scraped against her skin.

She deliberately edged away from the bed. "I want to talk to Parker." She commanded with more grit than she believed she had in her.

"They just left, but they'll be back soon enough," he squeaked. "He didn't think you'd be wakin' up so soon." The high-pitched voice contrasted the round, pockmarked face, and it reminded Millie of the shrill squeal of a pig. His thin hair, slick with grease, stuck to his shiny head, and Millie could see through the wispy beard that he had no chin. His head looked like a pumpkin on top of his scarecrow-thin frame, with one protruding tooth from his mouth.

"They?"

"Him and the woman." He reached out awkwardly, grabbing at her breast, but she dodged his revolting touch. She maneuvered the scatterings of broken whiskey bottles littered across the floor to get away from him.

He leered at her, and his empty eyes were terrifying as they stared boldly at the length of her. "They gave me a horse to let ya' stay here at my cabin. But I reckon that ain't gonna be enough. The rent's jes' gone up."

He moved closer, and Millie turned to run. His arm shot out, catching her around the waist and pulling her back against him. His body stench revolted her, and she fought the nausea rising from the pit of her churning stomach. Pinned against his filthy body, his face only inches behind hers, Millie gagged at the smell of his foul, rotting breath. She'd die before she'd let him molest her.

"Let go of me." She maintained control of her voice, masking her distress.

"He said I weren't ta touch ya', but I don't reckon I'll tell him." She could feel his small hardness between them, and her stomach turned over. His hand slid up to grope her breast.

Millie stiffened, as sudden anger and revulsion won out over fear. With strength and precision, Millie threw her head back, landing a shattering head-butt perfectly on his thick, bulbous nose, no doubt breaking it. Blood sprayed, and he released her, howling in pain from the blunt force. She had to act while he was still dazed from the first blow. Taking careful aim, she hooked him soundly in the groin with the toe of her foot, causing him to fall to his knees with a loud curse. As he fell, she brought her knee up with all the force she could summon, catching him under the chin and sending him sprawling backwards to the floor.

His head landed with a thud, sending up a light cloud of dust. Millie took a deep breath. She had to incapacitate him if she had a hope of escape. He tried to get up again.

She walked around him and kicked him as hard as she could to the side of his head, wincing with revulsion as she did so. He fell again, and she kicked him again, this time in the gut. Tears rolled down her cheeks, but she kicked him again in the head.

Seeing he was semiconscious, she ran, heading first for the woods, until out of the corner of her eye she spotted Outlaw. They'd stolen her horse, too.

"How considerate, you bastards." She choked slightly on the profanity. She was used to hearing Grammie swear, and though she swore little herself, she supposed the situation called for it. She wiped her eyes and ran to her horse. Climbing on his back, she took off in the direction of the midmorning sun, uncertain in her route, only knowing she had to move.

Once on her way, she leaned down, wrapping her arms around Outlaw's neck, wanting to give in to her tears. Gathering her emotions, she promised herself she would have a good cry when all this ended. She sat up to estimate her surroundings.

As the sun rose higher in the sky, an overwhelming feeling of despair consumed her. After traveling a short distance, it became clear that her horse was lame. She couldn't ride him a step further without possibly causing serious damage. He'd started out with a slight limp only a bit into her ride, but now he couldn't use the leg at all. She dismounted and bent to look at the swelling which traveled up the leg to the knee and noticed for the first time his bloody prints in the dirt. She lifted the leg and observed increased swelling and blood in the sole of his foot. Releasing the injured limb, she stood, feeling totally defeated.

Dropping the reins, she nuzzled Outlaw's neck and

face to hers, not knowing what to do. She feared the man would follow, and he most likely knew these mountains. She didn't. But she had to force herself not to think about that. She needed to find a way down out of these mountains and back to Raine's protection.

The sounds of the forest were unsettling for someone who grew up on the plains. Taking a deep breath, she sat down to weigh her options. She had to think calmly and logically about her situation, starting with the horse's injury, the crux of her dilemma. Who was she kidding? Everything was wrong, his sore foot being only one of many problems she had yet to face.

As a slight breeze ruffled her hair, the unpleasant smell of a dead animal nearby invaded her senses. She shook her head. Reassuring herself it was a different scent than that of the man who'd just assaulted her, she tried to concentrate on tending the injury and getting started before night came or someone found her. If something had become lodged in his foot, she could dig it out. She could lead him back down, and maybe, without her weight, he could walk.

"What is that smell?" She put her arm over her nose and looked back accusingly at her horse. To her disbelief, he dropped to his knees and onto his side.

"Outlaw!" she cried, scrambling to him. She touched his leg again and realized that it burned with fever. His breathing labored, he thrashed his head as she spoke softly to him. Loosening the cinch on the saddle, she let it roll off the other side of him. She looked about nervously, glimpsing a movement downhill several hundred feet. Her heart beat wildly. She sprawled over Outlaw's stomach to retrieve the knife off the saddle.

She turned back, seeing the movement again, but

she couldn't make out anything through the thick stand of trees. Panic rose in her throat like bile, and she tried desperately to get Outlaw to stand, pulling wildly on his harness. As she looked back through the trees, she viewed the figure, coming closer at a rapid pace. She could make out a horse and rider clearly now.

Suddenly, Jack crested the hill and ran straight toward her. Raine appeared next. She exhaled a trembling breath, but as soon as she observed his face, relief fled. Something was wrong, seriously wrong. The closer he came, the darker his scowl, and he fought for control of his spooked mount.

"Millie, come here."

"Raine, what's wrong?" She shook her head, confused by his sharp tone.

"Now!" he bellowed.

Millie jumped at his loud command, but just then the odor from before became overwhelming. Her curiosity won out over Raine's anger, and she turned. When she did, the breath left her lungs in a forceful whoosh.

"Millie!"

Common sense told her she should turn and run to Raine, but she couldn't move. Up the hill loomed surely the largest, most terrifying animal on earth. Standing on its hind feet and filling the sky, it roared with deafening ferocity. It was a bear, a grizzly. The beast was all teeth, all claws, and all noise, and even as far away as he stood, the grizzly seemed to surround her. Her blood stopped flowing for a few suspended moments before the pounding of her heart pushed it through her body with heated force. She began shaking uncontrollably.

She clasped her hands over her ears to shut out that horrible roar, but otherwise she stood frozen with fear.

Outlaw frantically tried to get to his feet. Beside her now, Raine gripped her arm and scooped her up. She slammed against the side of Raine's horse on her ascent, and then against Raine's iron chest.

Regardless of Raine's embrace, she would soon be dead. No one could face something so terrifying and live. Millie couldn't take her eyes from the bear, still looming above her on the hill, as he stood his ground, bellowing the blood-curdling growl. In only a matter of moments, the bear would charge.

****

Outlaw, sensing the immediate danger, struggled to stand. They rode away from the bear, picking through underbrush and fallen trees. However, the injured horse in tow slowed their descent down the mountain considerably, and Raine made a swift decision.

"We have to let go of Outlaw," he told her, despising the idea of leaving the horse. His arm closed around Millie's waist like a steel band, and his words warned no argument. "Keep going, no matter what. I'll catch up." He slid from the horse, and after a pleading look from her, he sealed his words. "Don't argue! Go!"

He grabbed his rifle from his saddle, and with a slap to his horse's hind end, sent her forward without him. Millie cried out, clutching the horse's mane for balance, and wondered where she could possibly go. Raine twisted the bit in Outlaw's mouth, causing him to fall easily back to the ground on his side once again. Shielding himself behind the fallen gelding, Raine tried to relax, taking careful aim.

The grizzly charge and Raine fired. He hit his mark, but his aim veered off marginally. Blood exploded from the bear's shoulder, but he didn't slow. The bear continued charging at full speed. Raine cocked the lever and fired another shot, again hitting his target, the expulsion of blood proof of his hit. But the enraged bear faltered only slightly before he began the charge again. Raine would be the bear's dinner in moments. Picking up a new rifle, he took careful aim and fired. This time skin and blood ejected from the bear's chest as the hollow point penetrated and exploded. The bear staggered toward Raine. Raine prepared to shoot again, but as he took aim, the bear fell only a few feet away.

Raine stood on wavering legs and examined the bear, making sure he was dead. Hearing a horse snort, he turned to see Millie standing behind him, frozen with fear, eyes wide, and mouth clamped in a rigid line, the pistol she'd taken from his saddle pointed at the dead bear.

"I thought I told you to get out of here."

"You did." Her knees went out from under her, and she sat down heavily on the ground. "Believe me, next time I'll listen."

"You could've been killed."

"Well, not necessarily. He would have gotten you first."

"And I suppose you'd have enjoyed watching him tear me to shreds? Could you possibly have worse luck? First kidnapped, then almost killed by a bear."

"Ha! I was just thinking you seem to tote disaster in your back pocket." Her voice shook, and he imagined it was laughter in her voice.

"Don't you have enough sense to realize how close we just came to being killed? Don't you have enough sense to be afraid?" he shouted.

Lying flat on her back and staring at a brilliant blue

sky, she answered shakily, "Believe me, I was afraid. If my legs were working at all, I'd get up and faint to prove it to you."

He paced, his fingers raking through his hair. When she smiled, he sighed. "What could you possibly find amusing about any of this?"

"You." She still stared at the sky, a tremor of shock rolling through her. "You're getting so worked up. I didn't know you cared."

"It's my own hide I'm concerned about." He dropped to his knees beside Outlaw, lifting his foot, prodding the meat of the hoof with his finger to find the problem. He pulled the knife hanging from his belt and dug. He looked at Millie, now sitting up, and his anger lessened. She had to be the bravest woman he'd ever met.

"Are you okay?"

His words were soft and gentle. Millie looked at him curiously. She seemed surprised by his concern.

"Yes," she croaked, her voice failing her. The impact of the events and the fear she'd been suppressing for the last few hours washed through her all at once, and she trembled.

"You have blood on you." Raine ran his finger across his own cheek, indicating the blood. She spat on her shirtsleeve and rubbed at the dried blood.

"It's not mine," she uttered. She scrubbed at her skin, her features twisted, fighting off tears.

"Want to tell me what happened?" Turning his gaze away from her, he began digging into the horse's foot.

"Later," she answered. She fought tears, but her distress was evident. "Is my grandmother safe?" she asked.

"Beauty is taking her up the mountains to my cabin. She'll be safe there." He held up a piece of glass, which had caused Outlaw's injury, but realized as she turned her face into the warm wind, she was close to crying. Guilt washed over him for being hard on her. She'd obviously been through a great deal, and he'd been incredibly callous. He wanted to take away her hurt, wanted to tell her everything would be okay.

As he studied her, not knowing what to do or say, he noticed fresh bleeding. Grabbing her bare foot in his hands, he examined it.

"We only have a couple of hundred miles left." He cleared his throat as he prodded her foot. "Do you think if we keep our fingers, toes, legs, and eyes crossed," he pulled a long splinter of glass from her foot and showed it to her, "we might possibly get through it without any further disaster?"

She smiled up at him and nodded, wiping away a single tear. Suddenly, a loud clap thundered in the sky, unseating Millie from her rock, and making Raine visibly jump. He rolled his eyes skyward, questioning what divine authority had sent him to such a fate. As if in reprimand for doubting a higher judgment, a bolt of lightning struck a nearby tree. In the commotion of the grizzly attack, neither had noticed the storm clouds rolling in with the wind.

"Where the hell did that come from? Come on." He grabbed her arm, pulling her up. "If we hurry, we can make it back to an old claim cabin I know of up here. It should be empty." He pushed her up on his horse. He climbed up behind her, and together, with Outlaw and Jack trailing, they headed back up the draw. Raine would soon need to tend Millie's horse, but his priority was getting out of this storm. With the luck they'd had so far on this trip, a lightning bolt was due to strike Millie at any moment, and there he'd be, sitting right behind her.

Chapter Fourteen

A warm, swirling wind caressed Millie's face and hair, and the now dark gray sky rumbled around them as they rode toward the cabin. Millie realized, as they traveled farther into the mountains, that Raine might take her to the same cabin where she'd been held up that morning. A tremble ran through her as she shared her fears with Raine and recounted her ordeal with the hideous man. The rolling thunder echoed her unease, but he assured her that no man would be a match for him in his current mood.

Despite the toilsome events of the day, Millie relaxed, felt almost giddy, so great was her relief to be in Raine's comforting presence. The notion that he'd come looking for her repeatedly voiced itself in her mind. Millie leaned back against him, lolling her head on his shoulder.

"How did you find me?" she queried, more to verify that he had been looking for her than actual curiosity as to his tactics.

His deep voice vibrated through her back. "I'm a pretty fair tracker."

"I've read that Indians can track anything."

"You read too much."

A soft smile graced her lips at his accurate depiction of her. "That's what Grammie always says." Millie relaxed, reclining against Raine comfortably. She became appropriately embarrassed, however, when he pushed her away from him.

Raine cleared his throat and changed the subject.

"Millie, how did they kidnap you?" The sarcasm in his tone betrayed the fact that he found humor in his next question. "Didn't you have your gun?"

Millie's blush deepened. She'd repeatedly told him how she could take care of herself. "Bridget drugged me."

"What?" he asked.

"I know it's hard to believe, but Bridget slipped something in my water. It was powerful stuff, whatever it was. I tried hard to stay awake, but it was impossible."

Raine remained silent for a long while, for so long, she turned to look at him, and upon seeing his odd expression, sighed, "You don't believe me."

He looked down at her with a strange light in his eyes.

"Yes," he croaked. "I do. But are you absolutely positive Bridget is in on this?"

She turned back straight in the saddle. "I can think of no other explanation. Believe me, I've tried."

"I hate to hear that," Raine features turned solemn.

"Me too. More than you could know."

Raine sighed heavily. "How am I going to break this to Tom? He doesn't have high expectations for his daughter, but I think this surpasses even his lowest. I have to find them. I can't go home without her, no matter what she's done."

Raine offered no further clues as to his intentions. The ride back to the cabin was slow, and the storm bore down upon them. An icy drizzle fell by the time they reached the rickety old shack.

As they arrived, Millie immediately recognized the place. Raine looked to her for confirmation, and she nodded, her somber expression letting him know this was the place. Broken glass and garbage marked the area as the same hole where she'd escaped from that morning. It rained harder, soaking their clothes, and Raine tied the horses a good distance away from the shack. Giving Millie a pair of worn leather moccasins to slip on her bare feet, he told her to stay with the horses until he returned.

"Not a chance," she answered, to which he frowned. By the squint-eyed "don't you dare leave me here alone" look she wore, it was clear intimidation would not work against her stubbornness. He motioned for her to keep quiet and follow closely. She kept a light hold on the back of his shirt, her anxiety about the horrid man inside eased only by her belief that Raine could protect her.

Still, she didn't want to let go of him even for a second, for fear she might get separated from him. Quietly, they crept up to the cabin. Raine listened carefully for any sound from inside but heard none.

He whispered softly to her, "Any chance you killed him?"

"I don't know. I've never beaten anyone up before," she answered.

He opened the door gradually, holding Millie back with one hand and holding his pistol in the other as he stepped halfway into the entrance. The rain came down in torrents, and without her hat, water rolled down Millie's neck and back, despite the makeshift roof on the porch. It took Raine what seemed like forever, and she couldn't imagine why. The ugly man was either in there, or he wasn't. Tension mounted as he stood motionless in the doorway, and a sinking sense of dread rushed through her when he stepped back out of the door and closed it.

"What are you waiting for? We're getting soaked." She reached for the doorknob to go around him, but he hooked her around the waist, stopping her. Putting her hand on his chest, she pulled back to look at him. The rain beat them soundly, soaking their clothes, hair, and skin. Water dripped off her long eyelashes, and his as well. They stood there for several moments staring at each other as the deafening drone of the rain surrounded them, intensifying the sound of Millie's heart thumping in her own ears. The pace of its beat increased.

She tried once again to pass him.

He barred her way and shook his head.

"You don't need to go in there." His voice tight and restrained, his words could barely be heard above the rain. From Raine's defeated expression, Millie discerned that he hadn't found the man from this morning, but someone else. She tried to make sense of Raine's grim expression.

A notion began to nag at the back of her brain. Neither of them had stopped to question Bridget's whereabouts. The subject of Bridget's involvement with Parker was a touchy one for them both, the sting of betrayal sharp.

Raine's defeated expression was severe as he pulled the door closed behind him.

"What?" She thought she knew what he would say.

"It's Bridget."

She took a deep breath and sighed. Her heart was pounding in her ears, and she couldn't accept all that had transpired, what she knew lay on the other side of the door. "Let me go to her," she pleaded quietly.

Relenting, he bowed his head and released his hold

on her. Millie entered the cabin and spotted Bridget on the rumpled old bed where she herself had awoken this morning. She lay partially covered, which didn't seem in consideration of her nakedness, but because the covers fell that way when she was killed. Millie went to her and brushed the brown hair away from her face in a tender gesture. The barely discernable bullet wound was in her chest, and even the minute amount of blood made Millie's stomach churn. She carefully pulled the blanket over Bridget, covering her completely. When she did, her derringer, the one Bridget had taken the night before, fell to the floor. Millie bowed her head as tears fell unchecked down her cheeks, and she whispered, "I'm so sorry, Bridge."

"Millie," Raine said softly. "She was probably in this thing from the beginning."

"I know." She wiped the tears off her cheeks and stood. "But I should have known. I should have done something." She held out the small gun to Raine. "He killed her with my gun."

"Parker?"

Millie turned to look at Bridget, lying naked under the filthy blanket, and turned back to Raine, pain twisting her face. She choked on her words. "God, I only hope so." The image of the man she'd fought off caused a clenching in her gut.

She shook her head and looked again at Bridget. Her words came out softly, mostly to herself. "She didn't stand a chance with Parker. She wasn't strong enough to go against someone like him, even if she wanted to. Maybe she tried, and that's why he killed her."

Raine searched Millie's face. His brow knitted with anger, and he shook his head.

"I don't know. Everything indicates she was a willing accomplice. But what kind of coward kills a woman, for any reason? This Reynolds must be a real sweetheart."

Millie rolled her eyes and wiped her nose on her sleeve. That action brought a slight, sad smile to Raine's lips. She reminded him of a child in so many ways, especially her naïve and tender heart. He wanted to protect her from further hurt.

"Her body's still warm." Millie sniffed loudly again.

Raine looked out the window, clouded with filth. "He could still be in the area."

"We still might catch him," she speculated hopefully.

"We? Not on your life. I wouldn't risk it. And I won't leave you here alone. We'll have to wait for another time."

Millie nodded, too tired to argue. She didn't think she could face anything else today, anyway.

"We should bury her." Raine normally wouldn't have bothered. He would have left the body for the animals to feed on, no less than she deserved for her hand in this mess, but this was Tom's daughter. He rubbed his tired eyes.

"I'll start digging."

"I can help."

Raine nodded. Taking her hand in his, he looked at it tenderly. He wondered if he, too, could have prevented the girl's death. Something deep inside told him he must protect Millie above all else. Looking into her tear-brimmed, green eyes, he deduced that keeping her safe for the rest of the trip would be essential to his peace of mind.

The guilt of her charade thundered through Millie, suddenly sickening her in the wake of Bridget's death.

"Raine, I need to tell you something."

He turned her hand over in his own and ran his finger across her palm.

"Raine?"

"Millie, I'm going to marry you."

Millie stood speechless for a moment. "Raine, I'm Thomas's daughter."

As he digested her words, Raine gave her a reproachful frown.

"I'm Tom's daughter." Another look from him, and she knew he didn't believe her. He damn well didn't believe her. "But I am." She supposed it made more sense for him to believe she lied now than that she'd been lying all this time. There would be greater benefit for her if she claimed to be the rich rancher's daughter now. But damn his eyes for thinking the worst of her. She didn't want to admit that she really couldn't blame him.

"Let's start digging." She turned and walked out the door, stopping on the porch and squinting up at the sky. The rain had not let up. The sooner they buried Bridget, the sooner they could get out of there.

Once they began digging, they found it to be a slow process. The rain rapidly saturated the ground, and sliding mud replaced each scoop of dry dirt they exhumed. It became a slow and frustrating process, but each delved into the chore with a tireless energy, wanting the job completed.

When the hole was sufficiently deep to see Bridget buried, Raine wrapped a blanket around Millie's aching shoulders and planted her underneath a tree. The sky had cleared, leaving the air crisp and cold, the late afternoon sun providing little warmth. He carried the body to the hole and placed it in the grave. Covering Bridget with the heavy dirt, he smoothed the ground at the site as best he could, then removed his hat, which Millie imagined was out of respect for Tom, more so than Bridget.

They left without a word or a backward glance, wanting only to get the place and day behind them. Millie sat up straight in the saddle until, perhaps sensing her exhaustion, Raine pulled her back against him and wrapped his arms securely around her. Riding for several hours in silence, they stopped only when the light of the day disappeared. Raine gathered wood for a fire while Millie laid out the bedding. Neither ate nor spoke, but both warmed themselves by the fire and drank heartily of the water Raine had managed to get from a spring near their camp. When Millie could no longer hold her eyes open, she looked at Raine and bid him goodnight, her voice broken with fatigue. She lay down on her pallet, her back to the fire, and finally allowed her tears to flow.

****

Raine stayed awake long after Millie had cried herself to sleep. He fixed his eyes on the campfire, straying only occasionally to glance at Millie's sleeping form. When he did, his pulse beat to the rise and fall of her chest. He felt ten times a fool. Could she be involved in this scheme against her grandmother? Raine looked at her and sighed. He should be angry at her for suddenly claiming to be Tom's daughter, and he wondered why she had changed her story when he'd mentioned marrying her. Maybe she hoped to deter him so she could carry on her plans with Parker Reynolds?

And then there was the question he didn't want to face. Had she killed Bridget?

Raine rolled onto his back and stared blankly at the star-filled sky. It would be dawn soon, but no revelations emerged about why Millie's boyfriend, or Bridget's lover, would go to such lengths. How rich was that old woman? And what were their plans to get their hands on the money? There were a few avenues he could explore for clues. The old woman's will, for one. And while he had the chance, he supposed maybe he should check out Tom's as well. How would he prove Millie wasn't Tom's daughter? Well, the old woman would know. Maybe that's why they wanted her dead before they reached Tom's ranch.

But the notion reverberated through his brain: Millie couldn't have had anything to do with this. Maybe he just didn't want to accept the possibility of her involvement, but Millie's relationship with her grandmother was genuine. Millie was genuine. He believed that, if nothing else. So why would she lie about being Tom's daughter? He'd longed for his actual parents often enough when he'd been a boy. Maybe it wasn't too hard to imagine she wished she had a father like Tom.

Anger flared within him as he contemplated Bridget's murder. He'd failed Tom in bringing his daughter back to him, but she'd obviously been in way over her head. He couldn't possibly explain that to Tom without sounding as if he were making excuses for failing to bring her home. Worse was knowing Tom wouldn't blame him, no matter how much of the blame he deserved. Guilt washed through him as he looked across the fire at Millie. If he hadn't been so preoccupied with her, perhaps he could have seen the danger Bridget had been in.

Millie stirred as she rolled toward the fire and

snuggled farther under her blankets. He studied her sleeping face, so delicate without the fire in her eyes shooting sparks at him. Her long, dark eyelashes lay gently on her flushed cheeks, and in sleep, her full, sensual lips made her look like a seductive woman, not the girl he'd befriended. She'd touched his heart like no woman had. He cared for her, a realization which surprised him.

But a ball of doubt about her true motives formed in the pit of his stomach, making his body ache. Something clouded his judgment with Millie, and he doubted his own sanity for not accepting that she could be a part of this entire plot. Maybe now they were not only after the old woman's money, but Tom's too. Why else would she suddenly claim to be his daughter?

Raine closed his eyes and shook his head once again in silent denial. He refused to believe Millie was anything but what she appeared to be, what he wanted her to be. Otherwise, how could he have fallen for her so easily? It was at that moment the realization hit him like a bucket of cold water. He had indeed fallen for her.

Chapter Fifteen

Raine sat up so suddenly he startled Millie as she rummaged through his saddlebags. He hadn't slept long. His movements had woken her only an hour or so before. He scowled at her and lay back down on his bedroll, facing the fire she'd just rekindled. He closed his eyes again, no doubt drifting through the tunnels of slumber. She sat down heavily and sighed. He raised up on his elbow and scowled again.

"Do you always sleep so late?" she asked him.

He turned and laid back down with his back to her.

"Raine, I'm starving. I've never been an entire day without eating."

He grunted. "I can believe that. I've seen you eat."

"Didn't you bring any food with you?"

Raine rolled back to look at her. "There's some jerky in my pack."

"Jerky," she responded lifelessly while staring at his broad back. "Jerky?"

"Jerky," he confirmed, his voice husky from fatigue, as he laid back down.

She sighed again, but he ignored her. Knowing he would need at least a few hours of sleep if he was to be a tolerable traveling companion, Millie decided to take matters into her own hands. She took his rifle and decided to find food for herself.

An hour later, she shot her prey. She carried the

rabbit in hand as she walked the short distance back to their camp, Jack at her side. She almost crashed into Raine as he charged into the woods with purpose. He stopped short when he saw her.

"I saw a deer." She indicated the woods behind her with a jerk of her head. "Which might have been better, but I didn't want to waste all that meat." She handed him his rifle as she walked past him. "Good morning." She offered over her shoulder.

"Can you dress that?" he asked, following her back to camp.

She didn't answer him. She squatted next to the dwindling fire and stuck his knife in the rabbit's underside, carefully making several incisions, and then skinning it. "Don't you have any normal bullets? Those things blew his head to pieces."

"I hadn't planned on hunting rabbit when I set out yesterday."

She carefully cut the rabbit down the center of his belly.

"Just other types of vermin. Are you okay this morning?"

She looked up at him, pleased he considered her enough to ask.

"Yes. I'm fine," she answered. Exhausted from an overly emotional day, she couldn't prevent the crying which had consumed her the night before. She'd tried to be quiet, but he had to have heard her. He'd left her alone, out of consideration she assumed, not out of the contempt a man might feel at a woman's tears. When she'd lulled herself into a peaceful state, and Raine had believed her asleep, he'd walked around the fire, and adding his blanket to hers, pulled the covers up around her shoulders. The gesture helped to further ease the turmoil inside her as she drifted off into a deep slumber.

Energized and excited this morning, Millie realized they would soon be at her father's ranch.

Hungrier than either of them realized, they ate their meal enthusiastically. Both grabbed for the last piece of meat, but Millie reached for it first, and Raine let her have it, shaking his head in amusement. He packed up their camp while Millie sat licking her fingers.

"Ya' know, I think I could've eaten that deer," she teased.

"I have no doubt." He tied the bedroll to the back of his saddle and checked his pack several times.

He turned to her. "Are you ready?"

She nodded.

He mounted his horse without another word and pulled her up in front of him. They rode for several hours in silence. The extra burden on the horse created a slow pace for them, but the day passed fleetingly for Millie.

She thrilled at the beautiful scenery as it passed before them. She wondered at the awe-inspiring view, the snowcapped peaks, as they traveled through the grassy plains. The next day, she lusted for a dip in the crystal-clear mountain lakes surrounded by craggy canyon cliffs they passed through, but she didn't dare ask Raine to stop. She could never grow tired of looking at golden aspen leaves against the deep blue sky, or breathing the dry, cool air.

Conversation between the two was limited, purposefully never turning personal. Millie didn't mind. Raine fascinated her with the detailed history of the area, the abundance of varied wildlife, and stories of the natives, explorers, and settlers of the territory. It suspended time for her, and at one point in the day it occurred to her that this had become, in some ways, the adventure she'd always longed for.

Because of their late start that morning, they rode long after night had fallen, the full moon providing enough light for them to continue. Raine wrapped a blanket around them to shield against the cold night air, which had descended upon the mountains.

Millie once again rode with Raine on his horse, and oddly enough, she sat perched comfortably in front of him. It seemed the most natural thing in the world to lean back against him. Her head fit easily under his chin, and the curve of her back rested comfortably against his chest. When he wrapped his arms around her, she sighed, feeling contentment engulf her.

She dozed for a while, feeling safe to do so in the protection of his strong embrace. She drifted in and out of a peaceful state of slumber. Awakening gradually, she became aware of the warmth of Raine as his body enveloped her and the unmistakable evidence of his arousal.

Thanks to Grammie, she was not unaware of how a man's body worked, but up until she'd met Raine, she had always deemed the reproduction process purely functional, uninteresting, almost humorous, at best. Whenever she'd considered any man as someone she might take as a husband, she only had to picture him in such a state of arousal, and she found her interest waning. Even Parker, as handsome as she'd once believed him to be, and as hard as she'd tried to like him at first, he still became a casualty of the less than flattering bend of her imagination. Whenever she'd contemplated the prospect of "making love" with him, she'd made a tight face instead. When he'd asked why she grimaced, she'd found it hard to contain her humor.

But now, feeling Raine's evidence of desire pressed against her, her blood pounded through her veins in a pulsing rhythm. Her senses, intoxicated by the smell of him, the warmth of him, the hardness of his muscular arms and legs as they surrounded her, ignited her body with awareness.

The saddle creaked and moaned as they plodded along in the moon's bright light. Millie pulled the blanket tighter and took a deep breath of the brisk air to calm the seething, which she recognized as her own desire. But when the heat of Raine's breath grazed her neck, she couldn't help but snuggle back against him, as if she could possibly get closer.

His lips were beside her ear now. "Stop squirming," he whispered tightly to her through clenched teeth.

A whimper escaped her parted lips, her consent to his command. He couldn't have asked for anything as difficult. She tried to still the throbbing of her own body. She groaned involuntarily and turned her head only a little, but it was enough for him to meet her lips with his. His hold around her waist became like steel, and his kiss commanded her into complete submission.

She didn't notice when the horse stopped, but Raine told her to get down, and she did. Trembling and taking a ragged breath, she dropped to her knees, then turned and sat on the slight hillside covered in soft grass. She watched him dismount and drop to his knees in front of her. Placing a hand on either side of her, he leaned forward and continued their kiss. She lay back, and he descended toward her, resting his weight on his elbows, and wrapping his hands in her hair. He kissed her, communicating his desire in it. She matched his fervor. His lips left hers, traveling across her cheek and down her neck, making her tremble with desire.

"Are you cold?"

"Are you kidding?" She exhaled shakily.

Raine's laugh came from deep inside his chest. He brought his face before hers and gazed into her eyes. Giving her a warm smile, he placed a brief and gentle kiss on her lips. He raised himself slightly, then after a moment's fumbling, he swore and rolled off her. Sitting up, he muttered under his breath, "Damn boots."

Millie laughed, enraptured by his effortless charm.

Raine yanked his boots off one by one and dropped them down beside her, smiling knowingly at the moon.

There should have been sparks where their arms touched when he lay down beside her. His voice, deep and silky, swept gently across her skin. "Millie…"

She looked over at him, and he continued staring at the moonlit sky above. "We're getting married tomorrow."

She scrutinized his chiseled profile. A tumbleweed of theories and emotions spun through her mind. He didn't believe her about being Thomas's daughter, and there might be hell to pay when he realized the truth. But she'd endure hell to be near him. Parker's manipulations still needed a counter solution, Bridget's murder crystalizing the urgency for it. Getting married would temporarily fix the problem, but with larger repercussions for her heart. One obstacle at a time. "If you say so, Raine." At the moment, she couldn't think of anything else she wanted beyond him. Everything else could wait.

His gaze locked with hers and he hesitated only a

moment before he rolled on top of her and kissed her lips gently. She absorbed each ensuing kiss as he placed them on her eyelids, her cheek, her ear. He lowered himself, kissing her neck. Unbuttoning her blouse, he kissed the swell of her breasts, then down to her stomach, he kissed her navel and the skin just at the top of her pants as he unbuttoned them.

Millie moaned, urging him not to stop there.

He sat up, and removed one of her moccasins, then the other, caressing her feet and ankles when they were bare. Sliding his hands halfway up her muscular calves, the passion smoldering in her eyes surprised him. Leisurely stalking the length of her, he kissed her mouth again.

With trembling hands, Millie unbuttoned Raine's shirt and pushed it off his shoulders, aching to touch the warmth of his skin. He tugged on her pants, and she lifted her bottom, allowing him to slide them off her easily. Then she wrapped her arms back around his naked torso, feeling the strength of his powerful body.

Raine kicked his own pants off effortlessly and placed a naked thigh between her smooth, silky ones. A tremor coursed through his body at the feel of her soft skin against his, of her taut belly against his. He groaned and buried his face in her neck, but pulled away, bringing his face before hers. As he looked into her eyes once again, the trust he found there unsettled him. He was being totally selfish in taking her; his conscious niggled. But he couldn't stop now. Nothing could alter the events and desires which had led them to being there, naked, wrapped in each other's arms, and he had to thank whatever fates, whether right or wrong, that led them to this.

He kissed her tenderly on the bridge of the nose. The better of his conscience prodded him to say, though not convincingly, "It's not too late. No damage has been done here." He looked down at her once again and glimpsed what looked like genuine hurt, but then her features relaxed, and she smiled as she slipped her fingers in his hair at the base of his neck and pulled his lips to hers.

It was all the answer he needed. He kissed her ravenously, then ushered wet kisses along the pulse of her neck. Cupping her full, firm breast in his hand, he lowered his mouth to it, taking the peak into his mouth and caressing the hard tip of it with his tongue.

Unaware of her response to him, Millie became lost in the heady urgency of what his mouth did to her, and the sensuous feel of his hard, naked body against hers. But Raine was all too aware. The feel of her confident hands exploring his back, her legs seductively intertwining with his, had him moaning in agony. Never in his life had he been so fueled in his passions, and never in his life had there been a greater need to do this right, to take his time and show her what making love encompassed.

Neither of them could touch the other enough, taste the other enough. The unexpected chemistry unleashed itself in their hands and mouths until they no longer needed to delay the inevitable. When Raine's hand slid between her thighs, Millie felt she would surely die from the ache he created deep within her, and she wanted more of him.

She gasped when he entered her, aware of the slight resistance on his first thrust. But soon, she arched against him, taking him in.

Raine was inside her, unmoving, not trusting himself to continue.

Millie moved restlessly under him, wanting something, but unaware of what it could be.

"Raine, I..." she began, but the words died on her lips, because she didn't understand what she needed to express.

Raine understood, and he fought for control over his own body, wanting nothing but to be able to fulfill her. His mouth covered hers, silencing her so that he could show her with his body, solve the mystery of her desire. He moved within her, and Millie responded by arching against him. Once again in control of both his conscience and his body, Raine began to move with purposeful strokes, and Millie fell easily, naturally, into the rhythm of his body within hers, as if his movements answered an age-old question.

Each movement of him within her caused her need to climb higher, a soaring longing for still greater sensations. She hung on the precipice as he filled her time and time again, until his pace quickened, and a crashing wave of sensation broke over her, exploding within her, finally extinguishing the fire burning within, as it washed over her body.

Raine's own lusts were satisfied as well, but with a staggering blow to his senses.

He rolled off her, pulling her pliant body against him. She wrapped her arms and legs around him, and he covered them both with the blanket. He couldn't speak. He could only stare up at the stars and the moon above them.

Both were silent for a while, content with the sound of the other's breathing, the other's sighs. The heat of their bodies fused their skins and separating themselves was unthinkable.

"I've never quite felt so…"

He had just been thinking along similar lines. "Quite so what?"

"The way I feel right now, the way you made me feel just then. Lying here under this sky with you, your body so warm, the air so cold and fresh." She inhaled deeply and ran her hand down his thigh casually. "I've never felt the way I do at this moment…that everything is right."

He hugged her to him and kissed her tenderly, the cool air making her mouth even warmer and more inviting. When he pulled away, she playfully bit his lower lip, and he opened his mouth wider, devouring hers again.

He groaned as he rolled on top of her, grabbing both wrists and holding them above her head. His elbows resting on either side of her, he looked down and smiled. "You've ruined it. You know that, I hope."

Even though the moonlight transformed everything to one hue of silver or another, Millie could still detect the blue of his eyes.

"Ruined what?" she asked, only a little afraid of his answer.

"This 'marriage', which will take place tomorrow."

"Oh?" She sensed his playful mood and moved seductively under him. "How so?"

He rested his head in one hand and twisted her shining curls around the fingers of the other. "You've ruined what was to be an ideal marriage, annulled as soon as possible, as all marriages between two people with any sense, should." He put his forehead to hers.

"But now…"

"Now what?"

"Now, I think annulment will be impossible. It will have to be a divorce. Definitely a divorce." He pulled away and looked into her eyes, and she lowered her gaze to his chin. She tried to make light of his words, as he had, but their impact brought a staggering realization upon her of how much she wanted, no, needed Raine in her life. He stared intently at her now, waiting for her to look him in the eye. When she did, the tenderness she found there surprised her.

She reached up, tracing her finger along the smooth scar marking his forehead.

He rolled from her and when he spoke, his voice held a harder edge than before. "What do you think?"

She climbed over to him and put her fingers over his mouth.

"I think I've never met a man like you, and I never will." She rested her forehead on his chest. "I'm sure you've been with lots of women, and things like this are easy for you, but I…" She wanted to express the raw emotions boiling inside her.

He put a finger under her chin and lifted her face to his. He scanned her face, noting the shimmer of tears only seconds before they dropped hot on his skin. He immediately regretted his words and tried to make them right.

"I've never been with any woman I intended to marry the next day." He pressed his lips to the top of her head.

"Now I've ruined it, haven't I?" he sighed into her hair.

She sniffed loudly and asked, "Ruined what?"

"Your perfect moment."

She pulled back to look at him. "No, you didn't. I did." She folded her hands on his chest and placed her chin on them. "I'm not good at saying what I mean," she offered. "I never had this problem till I met you. But now, every time I have something important to say, I mess it up."

He cradled her head in his hands, pulling it level with his and kissed her tenderly. "Then quit talking." When she broke away, he smiled. The face looking down at him glowed in the moonlight, and the mixture of moonlight and tears made her eyes glitter. Her hair hung in wild, curly torrents around her delicate face. Raine imagined she must surely be the most lusty and beautiful woman on earth.

She sniffed once more, then kissed him again, this time with a passion which surprised them both.

When their kiss ended reluctantly, he ran his hands down the length of her silky, firm body and rested them on her bottom.

"I think it's just a matter of speaking the right language," he said lustily. He kissed her again, positioning her on top of his erection. "You see? I understood that perfectly."

Chapter Sixteen

They weren't too terribly far from her father's ranch, and excitement, or perhaps apprehension practically rolled off Millie in waves. Was it meeting her father or the fact that they were getting married today that had her nervously fidgeting? Raine had decided not to say anything else about her claiming to being Tom's daughter, as much as it perturbed him. Besides, it didn't matter at this point. He was marrying her because of Parker, and that problem existed regardless of who she claimed to be. But he couldn't help the niggling feeling that he was missing some element of her declaration that might prove crucial in the long run.

She smiled at him and stood, wiping the dirt off her backside. "If it makes you feel any better, try reminding yourself that it's not a real marriage you're about to commit yourself to. I will let you out of it."

He took a deep breath and exhaled loudly, then mounted his horse. He didn't want to talk about getting married. He struggled to keep his composure, because he had the uneasy feeling this marriage might just alter the rest of his life.

Well, he wouldn't let it. It was just that simple.

Her nearness continued to stretch his nerves taut, so when she climbed up behind him, it did little to give him comfort that he was in control. It only confirmed his fear that this marriage could easily become more than in name only if he let his guard down for even a moment. He'd be lucky to get through one night without making love to her and satisfying the longing which seemed to settle itself deep in his soul.

"Thank you for doing this," she whispered, pressing her cheek tenderly against his back. Touched by her gratitude, his trepidation eased. Since he'd decided to go ahead with this marriage, he should buck up and try to take the ensuing consequences like a man.

He laughed out loud and grabbed her hand resting on his hip. Squeezing it, he wrapped it around his waist.

"What?" Millie asked defensively.

"What do you think your grandmother will say about this?" he asked, his humor high.

Millie groaned and boldly wrapped her other arm around him. "Believe me. You don't want to know."

"I need to send word on about your cousin when we get to town. Your grandmother and Tom should know, and the sheriff as well. Any other news can keep until we get there."

Millie nodded, her lips pressed together in a grim line.

As they moved closer to town, Raines's hands became tight fists, his agitation escalating as they reached the outskirts of Cheyenne. They found a church on the edge of town, and dismounted in the front churchyard, tying the horses loosely to a hitching post, allowing them to graze on the small patch of dried grass. Raine wiped his sweaty palms on his pant legs, cleared his throat, and regarded the simple plank church doors in front of them.

"There's probably another way," Millie offered. She looked at him with uncertainty. "You seem…doomed."

Raine gave her an appreciative grin. "No, this is the best way. And hey, it is only temporary, right?"

"Raine, I want to make you understand something."

He looked around, not really hearing her. Even here, on the edge of town, the streets were bustling with activity. He grabbed Millie's hand and pulled her around the side of the church. "That boyfriend of yours could be here in Cheyenne," he told her. "We'd better get this done and get out of here."

"But you don't really know who I am. I need to tell you."

He searched her green eyes, noting the challenge there. His eyes moved lower, resting on her lips, so full, so soft. But as he scanned her face, her flaming hair, spark-shooting eyes, and inviting full lips had the upper hand against his senses. He wrapped his hands in the silky auburn curls at the base of her neck and pulled her against him.

"I reckon I know you well enough."

He crushed his lips against hers in a passion-ruled kiss. He kissed her completely, until the ache for her became unbearable, and he pulled away. He rubbed his cheek against hers, and his warm, raspy whisper made her shiver as his lips grazed her ear.

"That may be the last time I get to do that."

Millie turned, brushing her lips seductively against his. "Goodness," she panted, "I hope not."

"Yeah, me too," he muttered. He brought his lips to hers, consuming her mouth once again. Millie ran her fingers through his hair, knocking his hat to the ground, and her mouth moved under his in a wild kiss, which had them both groaning with longing.

Raine reluctantly separated himself from her,

swearing softly under his breath. He stood for several moments with his arms wrapped around her. Eyes closed and lips pressed against her forehead, he held his body in rigid determination, finally prevailing over the madness which had consumed them both. He grabbed her arms and held her away from him. "Let's go."

Raine pulled her into the church. The minister didn't ask them why they were there. Raine thought that if nothing else, their flushed faces surely gave them away. The minister asked Millie if she wanted to make special arrangements such as flowers or a wedding dress. She assured him with a vigorous shake of her head that she did not. The pastor agreed to marry them and began the ceremony.

The words the minister spoke rang empty in Raine's ears as they echoed through the vacant church. When the minister asked Raine to state his full name, he replied "Raine McConnell". Raine looked to Millie, awaiting her turn, but her sudden expression of panic immediately set alarm bells off in his brain. A moment of complete confusion ran through him, blocking out all else. Something intangible was bearing down on him, although he couldn't identify the worry at first. Dread swirled like a tornado, becoming substance when the minister asked Millie to state her full name, and the moment at the cabin, when she'd claimed to be Tom's daughter, came back to him.

The minister bent to Millie, again asking her to state her name, but she only stared at the man, her features twisted in apparent torment. She swallowed, and replied, her voice coming out in a weak croak. "Mildred Carroll McConnell."

The short man ministering the service looked

between her and Raine, but apparently seeing no resemblance, dismissed their names as coincidence and continued his ceremony. But Raine couldn't grasp another word the man uttered as realization dawned. The moment he understood the entire implications of her masquerade, rage overtook him.

"I now pronounce you man and wife," the minister announced. At seeing the expression on Raine's features, he continued falteringly, obviously not expecting the groom to comply. "You may kiss the bride."

The minister hurriedly produced a marriage license, and Raine patiently waited for the papers to be signed. He ground his teeth as the minister's stout, well-meaning wife offered congratulations. Then he grabbed Millie's arm, dragging her down the aisle with long strides until they were out of the church and beside their horses. He unhitched both geldings and pushed Millie atop his horse, climbing up behind her.

They were on their way out of town before Raine had his temper controlled enough to speak. "Of all the lying, deceitful...Why I ought to...You little..." Raine sputtered, and Millie jumped in.

"I tried to..."

Raine stopped her. "Not one word. I don't want to hear any more lies." He pushed her shoulders forward off his chest. "I can only assume you were telling the truth, because I think even some of your more hardened criminals would feel a touch guilty about lying to a preacher. But I want you to know, I know you tricked me into this. I will not stay married to you."

Millie's anger reached a level matching Raine's. "If you think I want to stay married to you one hoot more than you want to be married to me, you flatter yourself.

And I did not trick you. I tried to tell you. If you weren't so stubborn…"

"I'm stubborn?" he roared. "God help me," he lamented as he looked to Heaven. "I am not the one who is stubborn."

"Yes, you are. You won't even listen to me."

"I refuse to be married to someone who has to argue with me constantly."

"I'm not arguing with you, you horse's ass. I'm agreeing with you. I don't want to be married to you." Millie scrunched forward in the saddle, trying to remove any contact with Raine. "This was your idea, let me remind you."

"This marriage will not be consummated, so do not, do not, go wiggling that behind of yours around in front of me. It won't work."

Millie groaned. "You're damned right it won't be consummated. If you could keep your hands off me, we would not even be discussing this. But let me assure you, that mistake will not be repeated." She turned, casting an incensed frown upon him. "And not once have I 'wiggled'."

"Now hold on just a minute. I didn't notice you recoiling in horror when I did touch you," Raine grunted. "I hope I'm not the one who must tell Tom he has such a bold and wayward daughter. He thinks you're an innocent young lady."

"Well, I was before I met you. And I'm sure he won't be terribly disappointed Bridget is not his daughter."

"Well, hell! At least a man knows what to expect from a woman like her!"

Millie turned to him again, eyebrows raised

147

expectantly. "Which is?" she demanded with dripping resentment.

Raine pondered her question for a moment and, shaking his head in defeat, he looked away. "Misery. The same thing you can expect from any woman. Damn it. How am I ever going to explain this to your father?"

Millie was clearly angry. But so was he.

"He'd like nothing better than to see us married. Now I'm going to get his hopes up and disappoint him all in one breath. Some friend I am."

Millie's expression of anger softened into a gloomy frown as she entwined her hands in the horse's black mane. "You're being a friend to me." She distractedly combed the bay's mane with her fingers. "Won't he appreciate that?"

"Damn it," he muttered. "I need to make a quick stop to send the news about Bridget to your grandmother. She should know. We'll head home immediately after that."

She nodded. The heat of her body against him made him agonizingly aware of the problem he now faced.

The silence built between them.

"Damn. Damn. Damn," he growled.

Chapter Seventeen

Later that night, only one thing could possibly be weighing so heavily on Raine's mind. He'd taken the truth of her deception much harder than she'd expected. He didn't look up as she approached. Cradling a bottle of whiskey in the crook of his arm, he drew patterns in the dirt with a twig in his other hand. As she reached him, his expression rivaled any the devil himself might have worn.

"Mind if I have a drink of that?" she asked.

He raised his head to look at her, cocking his brow over accusing blue eyes. "You're too young to drink."

"Well, it seems as good a time as any to start." Color rose in her cheeks.

Their day had passed in silence. Raine had displayed his anger with her whenever he delivered one of his fierce scowls. She regretted that the easiness between them before their marriage had now been destroyed. The wall of tension building between them unnerved her, and if the whiskey would help break a chip in that wall, she wanted to give it a try.

He gave her a skeptical glance and held the bottle out to her. She stepped forward, and careful not to touch his hand, took it from him. Her eyes locked with his, never faltering, as she took a large gulp. But she realized her mistake the moment she swallowed the burning liquid. Coughing to catch her breath, she looked at him through tear-filled eyes, expecting to see him laughing at her, but his expression had not changed. For a moment, she tried to hold on to the composure she had only just gained. However, feeling the whiskey warm her body, she relaxed and let out a little laugh. As if to further emphasize the fresh sensation, she expelled a mellow, "Whoo!" and sat down.

Raine still sat planted on the fallen tree, but now his angry scowl betrayed the fact that he thought she was being a fool. Feeling a bit of rebellion surface, she ventured to take another sip just to spite him.

"So what's wrong with you?" she sighed, not really needing an answer.

He raised an eyebrow at her. "Give me that bottle and go away."

She took another gulp, then handed him the bottle. He downed the mind-numbing whiskey with what looked like experience. Millie watched in awe as he swallowed a great deal of it without even a grimace. She set her task to portray such nonchalance on her next drink. She grabbed the bottle out of his protective clutches and took another swig. Her eyes squinted in their attempt not to water, but overall, she handled herself well.

Raine scowled even harder. "Ladies don't behave the way you're behaving."

"Good grief! What on earth is so great about being a 'lady'?" A small burp escaped her. "I've grown up around such so-called ladies. Do you want to know what I think of them?"

"No!" he cried. "Go away!"

"Where the hell am I going to go?" She had warmed to this cussing business. She sat looking at him, wondering what she could say to lessen his anger. As she watched the light of the fire dance on his face, her head became weightless, and her burdens lifted. Something else tingled inside her, a new feeling she couldn't entirely understand, but which willed her to scoot closer to Raine. When her knee touched his, he jumped as if burned, and went to stand a few feet away, on the other side of the fire. Her feelings hurt, but her determination fueled, she stood, keeping her distance from him, and held out her hand for the bottle.

"Can't you let me be miserable in peace? Can't you see I am trying to get drunk, and I'd like to do it alone?"

"Well, I want to get drunk, too."

"Then go get your own bottle," he snapped.

Millie burst out laughing at his indignation, and judging from the annoyance pinching his face, he didn't appreciate her mirth. "That won't be necessary," she slurred, repressing the giggles bubbling up. "It won't take me much more to get drunk, I don't think."

She swayed a bit, endeavoring to entice him with smoldering eyes. He raised the bottle warily to his mouth but immediately lowered it. His gaze became riveted on her lips. He moved slightly, drawing closer to her. She wanted him to kiss her. He was just about to, but he shook his head and broke the spell.

"It won't take you anymore, because I'm cutting you off."

"You don't like me," she pouted.

"I like you." He took a swig of the amber liquid, swallowed hard, and stared into the low burning flames of the campfire. "Maybe I like you too much."

"What does that mean?"

"It means you're asking for trouble when you stand

there and look at me like you want to be seduced."

She threw a stick into the fire, her bottom lip protruding like a petulant child's. "You're going to be a damned poor husband."

"How's that?"

"Because you intend to neglect certain aspects of our marriage."

"Let me remind you, we had an agreement. This marriage is not real." Bottle still in hand, Raine eyed her warily. "I will not have you dogging me till I'm worn thin with your efforts to seduce me."

She grabbed the bottle out of his hand. She took another swallow and shrugged. "Being that we're married, and everything is proper and all…Iss juss that I may never get another chance. And, honestly, I rather enjoyed it, though I sushpect I'd enjoy it just as much with anyone."

Raine scowled ferociously at her. "There is nothing 'proper' about that." He shook his head, as if to clear his thoughts. "We agreed to annulment. You're not backing out on our deal, are you?"

Duly reprimanded, because the notion had crossed her mind, she slurred her next words. "What's it exactly you're so mad about?"

"I'm mad because you lied to me. I'm mad because I unwittingly seduced my best friend's daughter. I'm mad because now I can't. I'm upset, because I've been dragged into something, and I have no idea what it's about. One person has been killed, two if you include that puncher in camp, and I don't even know why. I have never even seen the enemy; he's in and out like a ghost. Who is he? How many are there? What am I up against? I don't even want to talk about it! I have enough to worry about just getting you to your father and explaining this mess."

Millie bit her lower lip as she regarded Raine. He was angry at her, and though that was nothing new, now his anger seemed growingly personal. She watched him staring pensively into the fire.

"Raine, I love you," she croaked. Startled, he looked up. He squinted at her, blue eyes blazing with heat as he searched her face.

"I love you," she declared with sudden realization. *Why shouldn't she tell him? She wanted him to know.*

He smiled. "Millie, I should warn you, all first-time drunks think they are in love with everything." He took the bottle back from her and moved around to the other side of the fire again.

"Oh, hell, I know when I'm in love." She stood and turned her attention to the warmth of the flames. Holding out her hands to the fire, she took a deep breath. "Isn't this fire heavenly? I love thisss fire." Her words brought a hearty grunt from Raine, as Millie had just declared her love for the second time in a matter of seconds.

"Well, I do!" She laughed. Raine smiled again reluctantly as he took a hit from the almost empty bottle.

She playfully hit him in the shoulder with her fist. Laughing and holding up his hands to protect himself, he stepped away.

"Iss about time you smiled, you old goat." She followed him around the fire and hit him again, but this time, he grabbed her arm and pulled her to him. He kissed her as if he were starving for her, and she melted against him as her head began to swim. Heat spread through her limbs, but she shivered at the dampness left by his mouth as it explored her neck. His mouth found hers again, and she groaned involuntarily. The wet heat of his mouth against hers was the single, most sinful, hot, and wonderful sensation of her life.

****

As his kiss became urgent, his hands deftly unfastened the top buttons on her blouse. He pulled back and his eyes met hers, searching for hesitation on her part. Seeing none, he slipped his hand between the opening of her blouse, and as his hand touched her lightly bound breast, her body went limp against him.

Feeling her body melting with passion, he searched her upturned face and waited for her to open her eyes. He would not deny himself something they both wanted so badly. He was drunk enough not to care about the consequences. Her name rested on his lips, and he whispered it softly against her barely parted mouth. When she didn't respond to her name or his kiss, however, Raine realized why Millie had surrendered so thoroughly and had become a dead weight in his arms. She wasn't overwhelmed with passion. Much to his heated disappointment, she had yielded so obligingly because she had passed out cold.

With a heavy sigh, Raine accepted his defeat. Kissing her forehead tenderly, he scooped her up in his arms and laid her down on his bunk. He covered her with several blankets and turned to leave her to a peaceful sleep. Reconsidering, he turned back and bent to her, tucking the empty bottle in the crook of her arm, chuckling to himself.

"Mildred McConnell," he purred, imitating Tom's almost obsolete brogue, "Ye tempt me sorely, darlin'. What am I to do aboté ye?" He flicked a red curl off her cheek with a finger as he stared down at her sleeping form. He stood, finally, turning to find solace in the dark forest, because again tonight, sleep would elude him.

Chapter Eighteen

Millie woke the next morning to the drumbeat of her head. She opened her eyes at the nauseating smell of whiskey to find that she held in her arms the very bottle from which she had imbibed the night before. Had she gone to bed with that thing? Trying hard to recall the events of the previous evening, she didn't remember going to bed at all.

She remembered Raine kissing her and...please, no. Surely, he hadn't made love to her, and she didn't remember it. She lifted her blanket and sighed with relief that she remained fully clothed. The top few of her shirt buttons were unfastened, but nothing lay exposed, thanks to the tight cutoff chemise she always wore to conceal the fullness of her breasts. She climbed out from under the covers and warmed herself by the fire. Reaching over for her moccasins, she looked around the immediate area for Raine, and found him leaning against a tree, smiling infuriatingly at her. Jack, her no longer loyal dog, sat next to him with a look of disapproval on his wolfish features.

"How do you feel this morning?" Raine inquired glibly.

She groaned as she stood with the bottle in her hand. "I see Grammie in a whole new perspective." She tossed the bottle to him. "Nice touch."

"Hungry?"

She placed a hand over her vacant belly. "Starving. I think. Have you seen my dog?"

Raine laughed at the fact that her dog had finally taken to him. Raine held out a cloth with meat left over from the grouse they'd prepared the previous evening, but due to their lack of appetite, had left virtually untouched. It surprised Millie how good it tasted. She was so hungry she ate without stopping.

Raine leaned against the silver aspen trunk, legs crossed casually out in front of him. He was intently occupied at the moment, braiding long strands of horsehair, so Millie excused herself. She found a cold, fresh spring flowing out of the earth, and she used it to wash up and satisfy her deep thirst. Refreshed and able to face the day, she returned to where Raine sat lazily, braiding the strand. He didn't look up as she sat next to him and leaned against the same tree.

She picked a twig of sage and rubbed the leaves between her fingers. She closed her eyes, holding it under her nose, inhaling deeply and savoring the strong, fresh aroma. She leaned her head back and looked over at him.

"Are you still mad at me?"

Raine pondered for a moment, then shook his head. He glanced up, then back at his work. "Just tell me why."

He didn't need to expound upon his request. She'd been waiting for just this opportunity to recount the events which led to his misunderstanding of her identity. However, now that she had the opportunity, the words didn't come. She gave him a shortened version of the speech she'd rehearsed continuously until late yesterday eve.

"Grammie started it, obviously before I ever met

you. She seems to have a talent for creating trouble. What her reasons were, I don't know." Grammie would relish taking credit. After all, it had been her idea. But she could also not entirely blame Grammie. She herself had gone along with the scheme from the beginning.

As he reviewed his handiwork, Raine clearly expected her to continue. She threw the crushed sage branch in the dust and did just that.

"I just sort of fell into it after you were so rude to me that first time I met you." Her words held an accusation. She watched his expression turn sheepish. He realized his part in helping fuel her performance.

"You made me so mad that first day, it served you right to be at the end of one of Grammie's schemes. And I expected you to go panting after Bridget, which would have kept you away from me." She reached across and ran her hand under the pretty black and red plait he'd been creating. "But beyond any of that, I had my own reasons for not telling you."

"Tired of being an heiress?" He lay the strand down beside him and turned to look at her.

Millie sat up on her knees but wouldn't meet his eyes. "Yeah," she answered. She smiled, appreciating his insight and his willingness to listen. "It's sort of like people never letting you be anything but half-Indian when you know there's so much more to you. They expect you to live up to a part that has nothing to do with who you really are."

Raine understood all too well.

He changed the subject. "Millie, do you think you will ever want to go back to Kansas?

Millie shook her head. "Besides the ranch, I really had nothing there. This trip has been the only adventure

I've ever had." She gave him a hopeless "for what that's worth" wince, and he smiled.

"I've fallen in love with this country, even though I've yet to really have the chance to enjoy it. I do miss my friend, Lydia, though." She hesitated. "It really depends on my father. He may not want me to stay."

"Do you think he would send me all the way down there to get you if he didn't intend for you to stay?"

"He probably just wanted to get rid of you. You can be exceedingly disagreeable at times," she teased.

"And you and that grandmother of yours aren't?"

Millie laughed, but her mood abruptly turned serious again. She gnawed pensively on her bottom lip, a frown creasing her brow. "Raine," she looked up at him hesitantly, "do you think my father…?"

Raine watched the display of emotions on her delicate face, and he sympathized with her uncertainty. "Do I think your father what?"

Millie concentrated on the braided strand in her hands. "Nothing."

Amused and touched by her insecurity, he realized what she didn't. Tom would be proud of Millie, and Millie wanted to love her father, even if he turned out to be nothing she had hoped for. Fortunately, however, Tom was everything she could want in a father.

"He's going to love you," he prompted gently.

"I'm not what he's expecting," she blurted.

"No, you're not, and I can assure you, that will make him happier than you could know."

A rush of relief washed over her at Raine's words of reassurance.

Raine ventured to break the tension between them. "Do you know how your father came to own the ranch?"

When she shook her head, he continued. "He won it in a poker game from a man named 'Lazy Ace'. We couldn't help but wonder before we arrived what condition it would be in. Tom worried that the man's name might be an indication of the state of things."

Millie smiled. "And what state was it in when you arrived?"

"Let's just say, we had our work cut out for us." They laughed and the awkward silence descended upon them again.

Raine stood and began packing their saddles. Millie pitched in to do her share, as usual, but Raine, taking pity on her for her slight hangover, didn't rush their departure. Sometime after noon, they were under way. Outlaw's foot was healing, but still wouldn't tolerate Millie's weight, so she rode in front of Raine again. Jack had taken to following at a distance, seen only occasionally in and out of the trees like a ghost.

Rawlins was a full day's ride without stopping, and by nightfall they'd made good time covering the distance. A night in town would be best to rest and wash up before traveling the last few hours home. Besides, if his suspicions about Reynolds were correct, it would be in everyone's best interest that word spread, as soon as possible, that Millie McConnell had married, and to whom she was married.

Raine had always been an outsider, and he liked to keep it that way. And as people tend to fear the unknown, the people of Rawlins gave him a wide berth. Everyone respected and liked Tom, but they were wary of his much younger and mysterious partner. He sent Millie into the hotel with instructions to introduce herself as Thomas McConnell's daughter, and she and her husband would like a room for the night. Ned Smythe, the local hotel curator, would need no further information than that, to spread the word of Millie's arrival in town, relishing the tale, no doubt, with details of how she and her new husband shook the whole hotel with their antics. If only that were true.

Millie and Raine left in the shadows before sunup, and by the time they had reached the Lazy Ace, located in a valley at a somewhat higher altitude than town, a light snow had begun to fall. Raine took Millie directly to his cabin, which lay hidden in a stand of towering spruce. He found himself pleased by her reaction to their ranch. The hand-hewn log buildings tucked away between the majestic mountains surrounding their spread were of a different style than anything she would have seen in Kansas. The grandness and richness of the mountain terrain could be breathtaking even to him, who'd lived there most of his life. He never grew tired of the constantly changing light and landscapes of the land.

Once at the small cabin, Raine savored the reality of being home. It was time for Millie to be reunited with her grandmother, and he with Tom. And later he could sort out the mess he'd gotten himself into.

They entered the cabin, and a pair of probing eyeballs greeted them.

"Grammie!" Millie ran into her grandmother's arms. "I've missed you. I've been so worried about you."

"What took so long?" Margaret looked accusingly to Raine over Millie's shoulder.

"We did have our share of problems," he reminded her.

Margaret pulled back to look at her granddaughter. "So," she began as she scanned Millie. "You're good?

I've been worried. We received word of Bridget, and I honestly don't know what to make of it. I don't understand what's happened." Her voice cracked, and she sat down in the chair behind her. "You must tell me everything."

Millie looked back at Raine for reinforcement. "Grammie…"

Grammie cocked her head.

"We think she was working with Parker."

Grammie remained quiet for several moments as she searched Millie's face. Then she looked at Raine. "Parker Reynolds did this."

"I can't say for sure, but…"

"But nothing. It was him." She looked back to Millie. "Thank God you're all right, darlin'." She hugged Millie again, and a sob escaped her. "How did she get in the middle of this? Why would he kill her?"

"Oh Grammie. I'm so sorry." Millie began weeping.

Raine effortlessly ignited a fire in the potbellied stove while the two women comforted each other. He stood, watching as the flames roared in the stove. "Margaret," Raine said. "We'll talk."

Grammie pulled away from Millie and regarded him for a moment, then nodded her understanding. Millie gave him a look of gratitude before she pulled her grandmother back into her comforting embrace.

"I'm going to take care of the horses and then go on over to see Tom. I'll be at the house if you need anything," he told the women. "Take your time."

Neither woman acknowledged him as he left the cabin.

Millie stood in the center of the cozy living room as her grandmother began heating water on the stove. She admired the strangeness and luxuriance of the furnishings surrounding her. Richly colored carpets, obviously of native design, cushioned her steps. Weathered and worn moose paddles and elk antlers hung on the wall, while various furs and native woven blankets were thrown casually over the handcrafted furniture. The women stood there for several minutes, warming themselves by the stove against the autumn chill, each absorbed in their own ruminations.

"Millie. You should go see your father. But first, I have something for you."

Mille looked at the package, then at her grandmother. "What's this?"

"It's a dress I've been saving for you. I want you to wear it when you meet your father. You should dress for the occasion."

"All right, Grammie. Thank you."

"I just want to make things right," Grammie told her. "I need to make things right."

Chapter Nineteen

Raine looked back at Millie before leaving the cabin. An empty, edgy sensation churned in his gut. As much as he'd looked forward to the end of the trip, it also meant the end of his relationship with Millie. He'd never have imagined he'd feel such disappointment at the prospect. But Tom deserved better, and Millie deserved someone who would love, cherish her, and protect her. He was already proving to be a damn poor protector.

He walked to the doorway and looked back again at her standing by the stove with the old woman, clearly distraught about recent events, the wound opened again by sharing the news. He wanted to reassure her somehow but reconsidered.

Closing the door behind him, he walked the horses toward the stables, woke Jake Lansford from one of his usual morning catnaps, and after a hearty greeting between the two old friends, asked him to care for the two travel-tired mounts. The old man would treat them with special affection and see that Outlaw's injury would heal with the proper ministrations.

He turned eagerly toward the main house. Pulling cold autumn air deep into his lungs, a sense of elation washed through him at being home. Everything around him became new and pleasing to his senses.

And intertwined with all these sensations were images of Millie. He couldn't act as if nothing had happened between them, because it most certainly had. The truth of the matter was, he'd ruined Tom's daughter, and now he couldn't do the honorable thing and commit himself to her. It had become such a damned awkward situation. Millie was independent and strong, and frankly, he didn't know what she wanted.

How would Tom react to the news that he'd married his daughter? He could tell him it would only be a temporary situation, but he wasn't sure that was true. They needed time to sort it all out. Maybe the best thing would be not to mention it at all, yet.

Entering the expansive log home quietly, Raine shrugged off his coat and removed his dirt-brimmed hat. He walked to the den, where Tom sat in front of the fireplace, furiously puffing on his pipe. Raine stopped in the doorway and watched him. And he'd thought Millie was nervous! Suppressing a smile, he walked through and slammed the door behind him. Tom jumped up as if he'd just been burned by the blazing fire.

"Oh, Raine," he mumbled. "It's only you, lad."

"I've missed you, too," Raine replied with a chuckle.

Tom gave him a reproachful frown as he walked to the younger man and gave him a sound embrace, clapping him on the back. "It's good to see you, Son. I've missed the daylights out of you. Ya' look like hell though, boy. Was the trip so difficult?"

"We had a hell of a time, but that's a discussion for another time." Raine slipped the burlap bag he carried from under his arm and handed it to Tom. "And it wasn't easy getting this," he scolded, as he handed the package to him. The package was a bottle of fine Scottish whiskey, which Grammie had buried many years ago.

Tom was the only other person who knew of its existence. Raine could only imagine why Tom believed it was so amusing to steal Margaret's hidden stash.

Tom studied the bottle, the label long worn away.

"This was a gift," he told Raine as he uncorked the bottle and sniffed its contents. "I gave it to Margaret the day I married." Tom poured two portions of the amber liquid. "I'm sure she's forgotten it existed."

Raine shook his head, accepting the glass Tom handed him. "She doesn't strike me as one likely to forget where her booze is hidden."

Tom sipped the liquid, savoring its perfection. Rocking back on his heels, he queried knowingly, "And how did you find Margaret Carroll?"

Raine scowled. "Disagreeable."

"Yes, I knew you would. Delightful woman, isn't she?" Tom sobered, swirling his whiskey as he brooded over it. "And my daughter? Is she well?"

Tom surveyed Raine's expression for some clue, but his features revealed nothing. "Oh hell, Raine," he blustered. "Is she as bad as all that?"

Raine's brows drew together, but otherwise his face showed no expression. "I'll let you judge for yourself," he offered.

"You can tell me the truth, Son," Tom encouraged Raine to give something away. But as Raine still offered nothing. "Good God, man," he raged. "Does she have no redeeming qualities?"

Raine took a long draught from his glass, swallowing hard. "She's exceptionally beautiful."

Tom frowned at his adopted son. "You're not going to tell me, are you?"

"Nope."

"Damn you to hell," he croaked resentfully.

"You did that when you sent me after her." Raine conveyed his humor with his eyes and Tom relaxed a bit. He scooped up the bottle and nervously sloshed liquor in his glass, clanking the glass clumsily, and then refilling Raine's.

"What the hell happened, Raine? What is this business of the girl being murdered? Margaret was beside herself and ranted about this man Reynolds. Do you know who killed the poor lass?"

Raine's humor faded. "We'll talk about it later, but it's bad. Please don't ask Millie about it. I'll go see the sheriff as soon as Millie's settled."

"Millie." Tom chewed on the name and nodded but remained silent. A light knock on the front door interrupted Tom's reverie. It creaked open. Terror overtook Tom's features, and Raine stifled his urge to tease him about his fear of his own daughter.

Millie was nervous and Raine was glad. Otherwise, Tom wouldn't have stood a chance. Raine left Tom, disabled and helpless, and went to intercept his wife at the entrance, where she removed her cloak.

At his first glimpse of her, he too became paralyzed. He could only gape admiringly at the lovely image she created. The lavender silk dress her grandmother had chosen fit her curves perfectly. Nothing about the dress constricted or added to the perfection of Millie's shape. The womanly figure she cut in the simple gown, coupled with the slight swell of her bosom atop the fitted bodice, made his mouth go dry. He never could have imagined this little ruffian, who had more grit than a lot of men he'd known, could so easily transform into an elegant lady. He owed the old woman for this one.

Millie's light green eyes danced with anticipation as his gaze again scoured the length of her. There were tendrils of dark auburn hair still damp around her face from bathing, and her cheeks were flushed despite, or perhaps because of, the chill in the air outside. He'd seen no one as striking, and he'd have liked to puff his chest out with pride that she belonged to him. But she didn't. He moved to stand before her, out of Tom's sight, and he gave her his shot of whiskey. She turned it up, downing it in one gulp.

"Thanks." The whiskey made her voice tight.

His eyes raked her shapely body again. "You look so…" Never had a woman rendered him speechless before. "You're stunning."

She flushed, smiling up at him expectantly. "I look okay?"

"You look perfect." He leaned down and gave her a soft kiss of encouragement on the cheek, then straightened, affected uncomfortably by her beauty.

"Don't say anything of our troubles or the marriage to your father yet. Please? I'd like for your grandmother to be here, so we're all here when we explain what's going on." She nodded faintly, her happiness tainted by the mention of Bridget and their sham of a marriage. He took her arm in his and led her into the den, where Tom stood pacing nervously. Raine suffered no surprise when Tom turned, his mouth dropping open at the incredible sight of the woman before him.

"Tom, this is Millie," Raine prompted quietly as he pried her distraught grip from his sleeve and pushed her forward. "Your daughter."

Tom put his drink on the table and then fumbled awkwardly for something to do with his hands. He ran one over his thick gray hair and sighed. His complete attention finally rested on Millie, and his pride became evident. His shyness suddenly gone, he choked out his greeting, not the one he'd practiced, but the one which suddenly poured from his heart.

"Millie, I'd know ya' anywhere, darlin'. My own mother had hair that color."

Millie blushed at her father's intimate greeting.

Once again, Tom grimaced at her silence. "Millie, I know you've had a lifetime without me." He cleared his throat awkwardly. "I know ye canna love me overnight, but I hope ye can learn to love me, as I've never stopped lovin' you, since the day ye were born."

There was tenderness and sincerity in his eyes as he spoke the heartfelt words to her, and she ran to him, throwing her arms around his neck, as tears flowed down her cheeks and a wrenching sob escaped her.

Tom wrapped his strong arms around her and comforted her, as he'd dreamed of doing so many times, as a father comforts his little girl.

"Now, now, Millie darlin'," he whispered, "everything's all right now. We're together at last."

Raine quietly backed out of the room and waited just beyond the door. He remembered his own parents, their memory still painfully vivid, but he shook his head thoughtfully and smiled. He'd been proud to know Tom as his father. He was a grown man now, and Tom finally had his daughter with him.

After a short while, laughter on the other side of the door came to him, and then a rush of excited conversation. Raine pushed with his shoulder to right himself from his leaning position against the wall, where he'd been waiting to hear just that, and quietly exited through the front door.

Millie would stay in his cabin, giving her space and perhaps a little freedom. It would be the best gift he could give her. The bunk cabin was empty this time of year. He'd stay there. More than anything he looked forward to a full night's sleep. He suddenly couldn't remember having one since the day he'd met Millie.

Chapter Twenty

It was a grey, snowy morning when Raine knocked on the door of his cabin. They'd each spent the last two days resting and restoring themselves.

"Come in," she called. She sat by the window with Jack at her feet. The old woman had moved to the main house with the snow, and the cabin seemed smaller with just the two of them in the room. Millie ignored Raine, as well as the book in her lap, staring out the window with all the wonder of a child. The foot of snow, which had silently fallen over the last couple of days fascinated her.

"Isn't it beautiful?" She muttered, as if not to break the spell which held her. "I don't think I could ever tire of it."

She'd seen snow before, but never this much. It was magical. Everywhere she looked, a thick, heavy blanket of snow draped the scenery. Raine broke the quiet by asking, "Want to go for a ride?"

She looked up at him and his seductive smile gave her pause. Of course, she would give in and go with him. How could she refuse the invitation when he stood there looking at her with those lusty blue eyes? The fact was, she ached to spend some time with him. He'd been busy since their return, obviously avoiding her, and although her father was a charming and attentive companion, and her grandmother always a comfort, she'd missed Raine.

Still, she didn't want to seem too eager.

"Well, maybe," she conceded. "I've been inside the last couple of days, and I'm dying to get outside." She stood, perhaps a little too eagerly, and gave him an impish grin.

"Good!" He stood, eyes fixed on her face, seeming to take in every detail. "We'll ride the line and check the cattle."

She looked back at him, obviously befuddled. "You're serious."

"Of course." His expression turned to one of derision, and he chaffed, "Surely, you weren't imagining personal recreation when the temperature hasn't risen above freezing all day?" His mischievous expression made his innuendo clear.

Millie rolled her eyes and looked past him, refusing to give him the satisfaction of seeing her chagrin.

"You flatter yourself." Flushed crimson all the way to her red roots, she walked past him, grabbing her coat, shrugging it on. She turned the attack. "Is that all you can think about?"

Raine clearly had no intention of letting up on teasing her. "Me? Ha!" he shouted for emphasis. "Imagine, in this weather! You're not thinking of going back on our deal, are you?"

"You're out of your mind," she wailed. "Of all the conceited, infuriating…"

He looked down at her with mock reproof in his eyes. Then, grinning at her outrage, he leaned over to her, his lips against her ear and his breath hot against her skin. His warm body pressed close. Her breath quickened, and her heart began to labor in her chest. She stood perfectly still, eagerly awaiting the promise of his whispered words. When he changed his mind, however, and straightened, giving her only a lusty, maddening smile, she stomped her foot, gasping in frustration.

She didn't understand his need to provoke her. He tugged her coat securely around her neck, sufficiently bundling against the weather, and opened the door, leading the way outside.

Incensed, she stared at his back for a moment, then followed him out, slamming the door in her wake. She stepped off the porch, and her feet shot out from under her. The jolt to her backside as it landed hard on the snow-covered step took some of the bluster out of her, and she waited for Raine to turn and show his concern. Only her pride hurt, but some concern on his part, even if feigned, would have been nice.

He turned, scanned her from head to toe, and smiled. He winked and gave her a roguish leer. "Maybe later, sweetheart. After the annulment. Right now, we have work to do."

It took great will to not screech her fury at him. Ignoring his outstretched hand, she carefully climbed to her feet. He shrugged and turned once again to the stables. She walked behind him with short, furious steps, struggling for her footing in her slick boots. Scowling at him from under the brim of her hat, she watched his shoulders swaying as he walked, and admired their broad expanse. Her upper lip curled in a snarl at the back of his black head for causing her insides to flutter. She should want to do violence on his person for such fiendish behavior. And as much as she wanted to be mad at him, she found it becoming increasingly difficult as her gaze trailed the length of his powerful body, and what she knew lay under his coat, from his wide shoulders down to his narrow waist, over his taut rear and along his muscular legs.

As she watched him, she imitated the strong, purposeful stride of his long legs. Her mood lightened as she rapidly mastered the method, and the snow crunched dryly under her feet with each step. The cold lung-tingling air and the light thumping of snow on her hat ignited a peculiar thrill that washed over her. She'd experienced so many new and exciting sensations. She admitted the one burning brighter than all of them was being in love.

****

When Raine finally turned again to look at her, the simmering arousal of emotions revealed themselves in the smile she wore, causing his steps to falter. He stopped and turned full towards her. His eyes softened, and he opened his mouth to speak, but the words died in his throat.

"Come on," he croaked as he grabbed her gloved hand and gently pulled her along behind him to the corral.

He tried, he really tried, to keep his mind on the business of saddling his horse, but as he watched Millie, also going about saddling the now healed Outlaw, he couldn't help the direction of his thoughts. He found her so damned attractive, it became harder by the moment to keep from tumbling her to the ground. He wanted her badly. He ached with it. So, when he rounded the other side of his horse and brushed against her, despite his better judgment, he grabbed her elbow and turned her towards him, his mouth descending on hers with some eagerness. And it went against all he'd been fighting to preserve when he pulled her willingly into the stall and lay down with her onto the clean hay. Rational thinking abandoned him when he discarded their clothes like it was the middle of summer, and as if there wasn't a chance in hell someone could walk in on them. And damned if he cared that he shouldn't be making love to her. He wanted her, needed the feel of her against him again. And the thrill of his discovery that she wanted him, too, only fueled his lust. Later that evening, when they were leisurely making love in the cabin, the full realization that Millie had become his wife in every way struck him. And as much as he tried to feel despondent at the fact, he couldn't. He experienced only an uncanny sense of fulfillment. He could worry about the rest later.

Chapter Twenty-One

Raine entered Dixie's saloon in the middle of a cold, sunny afternoon. Most men who came through town ended up in Dixie's eventually, and Dixie had a keen eye towards her patrons. She noticed anyone that stood out from the hordes of miners and ranchers frequenting her place. Someone as slick as Parker Reynolds would surely stand out, which is why he sought her out today.

"Raine!" Dixie called from where she stood alone at the end of the bar. "Where've you been?"

Raine looked around at the men standing at the bar and scattered about the saloon, all harmless faces he recognized easily. Nodding to a familiar man playing cards, he then turned his attention to his friend. "Hello, Dix. Do you have a minute?"

"You know I do. Talking's all you ever want to do, anyway." Her attitude was good-natured, though a touch reserved. "I have all the time in the world to talk. Drink?"

Raine nodded absently and took a seat in the room's corner. Dixie followed close behind, carrying two glasses of whiskey, the bottle tucked under her arm, and placed them on the table. Pulling the chair across from Raine over next to him, she sat down and waited.

He pushed the glass around in a small space on the table with one hand while he deliberated how to phrase his questions in a way that revealed nothing. "Have you noticed a man in here, new to town, relatively slick, handsome, I suppose?"

"A city fella?" she asked. Raine nodded. Newcomers were common enough since the railroad had come, though they usually traveled farther west. Reynolds would most likely seem harmless enough to anyone who didn't know what he was capable of. Retying the bow on the front of her dress, Dixie shook her head. "It's been the same ol' crowd in here as usual lately." She changed the subject, not realizing the importance of the information Raine sought. "Where ya' been lately? I heard you went and got married."

Raine stopped, giving her a self-conscious grimace. He and Dixie had never been beyond friends, but she had feelings for him. He'd read it in her eyes whenever she'd looked at him, as she did now. For that reason, he never went near her bed. Scratching his head under his hat, he laughed. "As a matter of fact, I did."

Her mouth dropped open, but she recovered, clearing her throat to speak. "I'll be damned," she muttered. "Never imagined I'd live to see that."

"I'll bring her by to meet you sometime."

"Don't you dare," she objected stoically. "I'd much rather imagine what sort of ugly toad she must be."

"Ugly." Raine scrunched his nose in a sportive sneer. "Red hair, and a lousy drunk."

Dixie gave a small smile. "On second thought, maybe I would like to meet her at that."

Raine sobered. "I'm looking for this man, Dix, but I don't want him to know it. I think he's dangerous. He's blond, tall, mustache."

Dixie nodded.

"Stay away from him, if you can help it." Raine stood to leave and put his whiskey down on the table, tapping the glass with his finger. "Dix." When she looked up at him, he repeated softly. "Stay clear of him."

Dixie nodded perceptively. He picked up the glass, downing the contents, and placed it, empty, on the table. "Thanks."

Pulling his collar up against the clear cold, he stepped off the sidewalk, traversing the street to the sheriff's office. He entered, relieved to find Pete Carson behind his desk and alone. Pete didn't bother to look up from his paperwork, saying casually, "H'lo, Raine. I saw you going into Dixie's. I figured you'd be crawling up my pant leg next." He looked up at his friend and placed his pen on the desk. "How ya' been?" he asked with a smile.

"Has Beauty been by to see you?"

"Yep. Heck of a fellow," he said with a gentle laugh. "Nice guy, though. He dug up some good information about your man there. Tell me, what does all of this have to do with you?"

Raine ignored Pete's questions. "What's Reynolds's real name?"

Understanding Raine had no intention of giving up information, Pete sighed. "He has several he uses."

"Is he really even a lawyer?"

Pete grunted at the phrasing of the question. "Yes, but he's not one of your more respectable lawyers. Robbing grieving widows and riding on the wings of disaster is his style."

"Now murdering young heiresses," Raine muttered contemptuously. He removed his coat, tossing it on the bench behind him, and removed his hat, tossing it atop his coat. "Do you have a list of the names he uses?"

Pete handed him a sheet of paper that Raine studied

intently for several minutes. His brows suddenly shot up. "It couldn't be a coincidence."

"What?" Pete asked, not knowing exactly which name had caught Raine's eye. Since the first time Raine had come in and told him there'd been a murder, and his suspicions of the culprit, Pete had spent a great deal of time investigating the trail of one Parker Reynolds. With the help of John Reichman, or Beauty—an ironic name—he'd unearthed some solid clues. Pete stood and paced, pulling up his pants front and back with both hands.

"This may make several things clearer, but I need to find out more. He may have reason to kill again. I can't let that happen," Raine told him.

"Kill who, exactly?" Pete wanted to know.

"My wife."

Pete's mouth flopped open. For a man who was so diligent and thorough in his detective work, he remained blissfully ignorant of town gossip.

"Didn't know you had one," he offered hesitantly.

Raine ran his tongue along his lower lip, leaned back in his chair, propping his feet on Pete's desk, and folding his hands behind his head. "I met her in Kansas."

"Kansas, huh?" Throwing his hands up, he beseeched Raine. "Please tell me what the hell is going on, and what this whole thing has to do with you?"

Raine let silence fill the room. "She's a pretty little thing, red hair, green eyes." He smiled. Pete ground his teeth. "And she just happens to be Tom's daughter."

"Didn't know he had one." Pete's tone was dry. "Okay, I want to hear this story from the beginning. Leave nothing out. I want to hear it all. And most of all, I want to hear how this wife of yours...Tom's daughter?"

He shook his head. "How did Tom's daughter become your wife and the target of a killer?"

****

Raine left town and rode for the ranch. He needed to talk to the old woman. He wanted to see the end to this thing, but Reynolds had yet to show himself, and Raine had no proof against him. Maybe the old woman could shed light on Reynolds, and why she believed he'd chosen her family as his target. He had an inkling forming, but he needed Margaret's insight.

He'd never admit it to anyone, but he actually enjoyed the old woman's company. Since he'd moved her into Tom's house, he visited her often. Raine found that despite her eccentricities and her age, Margaret was enormously intelligent and sharp-witted. She was also a loving woman, as evidenced by the affection she held for Millie, and the genuine sorrow, which even *she* seemed surprised by, that she'd shown at the death of Bridget.

He knocked on the door of the darkened room. She looked up only briefly to identify her guest and bid him come in. She sat in front of the blazing fire, nothing but its glow for light, and he sat in the rocker next to her. The squeak of her rocker and the hiss and crackle of the burning logs broke the silence of the room. He was content to sit, absorbing the warmth of the fire for a few moments.

"He can't possibly think he'll get any money by hurting us now that we're onto him."

"His motives have gone beyond any logical reasoning, as far as I can tell. People like Reynolds believe they are invincible and entitled, which is why he is dangerous." Raine casually sat forward in the rocker. "But I need you to tell me, Margaret. Tell me what you know. Please."

Margaret squirmed in her chair uncomfortably, a frown playing across her brow. Raine watched her, noting her discomfort, and her frown deepened under his regard. Finally, she looked at him. "Maybe I can help." Then she looked away, and they rocked awhile, the creaking of the chairs echoing their movements. Raine gave her the time she needed to collect her theories.

"I didn't know any of this before this trip. But somewhere along the way, I started thinking about what he'd said. 'I know who I am, and I deserve my share,' he said to me when I told him I was taking my business elsewhere. 'When you die, I just want my share.' I assumed he was crazy, and I told him, 'Millie won't marry you, and you aren't getting anything, you crazy fool'."

"He went into the rage that nearly made me soak my bloomers. 'You owe me!' he shouted at the top of his danged lungs. I had no blasted idea what the hell he was talking about." Margaret's fists flew with no particular purpose as she related the story. "'You owe me!'" She rested her arms on the sides of the rocker and let her hands dangle lifelessly as she continued. "And then it hit me. Carl. He looked so like Carl at that moment, his face all puffy and red to the roots, spit flyin'."

"Carl?" Raine asked softly, for Margaret seemed to be in another world, and he feared he might startle her.

Margaret looked at him, confused at first, but then she came back. "My son."

Silence filled the room once again until Margaret heaved a sigh and enough wind into her lungs to tell the story. "I didn't even know they existed until the orphanage in New Orleans sent me a letter tracing me as the grandmother, and even then, they didn't mention a boy, just Bridget, because they couldn't find a home for a temperamental girl. She was about nine then. Millie would have been five."

"My son and I were estranged. He ran away young. He was a drunk and a gambler and about half-insane. A mean, mean boy. But Bridget was innocent, so I took her in and loved her like my own. But she was always a hateful child too, and nothing I could do would change her."

"You're saying that Bridget and Parker are brother and sister?"

Grammie nodded, letting Raine draw his own conclusions. "I didn't know. I only began to suspect when he sent me the letter. He would only think he had a right to an inheritance if he was blood."

"Margaret, what about your will?"

"I provided for both girls, though Millie would receive the bulk of my obscene fortune, only because she earned it. She worked hard all her life, and she's loved me like no one else ever has. I'm sure you can guess that is work in itself. Bridget's portion would have been in a trust, with Millie in control of it."

"I don't have any facts to tell me Parker is my grandson, only what's in my gut."

Raine sat back in his chair, the wheels of his brain grinding in the silence. Awash with relief, he began to understand. It was all making sense.

"I think I may have something that can clear that up." Raine handed her the list Pete had given him. "This is a list of Reynold's known aliases. Do any of those names look familiar?"

Margaret scanned the list. Her eyes snagged on one

name and widened. She looked back up at Raine. They locked eyes.

"Well, now I guess we know."

Grammie sighed heavily with the burden of her years. "Yes, Son. I suppose we finally do."

Chapter Twenty-Two

The days passed as the snow continued to cast itself peacefully over the land. Days turned into weeks, and weeks quietly vanished into months. Christmas came and went with little fanfare. The mood remained somber, uncertain.

Kicking the cabin door closed behind them, Raine followed Millie into the cabin with an armload of firewood. He tried daily to make sure she was comfortable and had spent a great deal of time helping her with everyday tasks which were a part of ranch living. She did not shy away from work or chores, but he was wrestling with a guilty conscience and endeavored to make things a little easier for her as she adjusted to her new life.

He'd been a cad that day in the stables and for the rest of that night. He'd taken advantage of her for his own greedy purposes and making it up to her would be crucial. He'd betrayed her trust, and the shame of it went through him every time she looked at him.

He had another worry which haunted him vaguely in the corners of his mind. Millie had placed her trust in him to protect her and her grandmother. Although, the precautions he'd arranged until this point probably had stalled Reynolds. Knowing what he did now, he didn't think for a minute that Parker would give up.

He watched Mille now, stuffing another log into the

stove, diligently fueling it until the fire cracked and popped, and the stove glowed cherry red with the heat it emitted.

"Millie, turn down the stove," he instructed patiently. But when she reached for another piece of wood, his tone became insistent. "You're going to burn the cabin down!"

"I'm freezing!" she cried, her voice full of panic.

"You're sweating!"

She stood, threw the log into the corner behind the stove and turned to him. "I don't know if I can take it."

"You'll get used to it. I promise. This is your first winter this high in the mountains. It won't stop snowing until April. Naturally, it's going to be tough."

Millie growled, snatching off her gloves and throwing them at his head. Chuckling, Raine swaggered self-assuredly over to where she stood and tucked an errant red curl behind her ear. He stared at that lightly scattered mosaic of freckles on her nose and resisted the powerful urge to kiss her.

"I'm going to get some breakfast," His voice turned husky, and he wondered why his heart beat faster. "Are you coming?"

****

"You go." She pushed him out the door. "I'll be there in a minute." Closing the door behind him, she leaned back against it, closing her eyes. Breakfast. Ugh! The mere mention of the word made her want to point her face towards something and hurl her insides at it. She closed her eyes against the suddenly oppressive heat of the room. She opened the window, drawing deeply on the fresh air.

Concern marking his brow, Raine stuck his head in

the open window, startling her. "Are you all right?" he asked.

"I'm fine," she assured him. "I'm just not hungry, that's all." She abruptly closed the window in his face, so he'd go away and ask no further questions. He conceded, strolling away, and she opened the window again for a fresh breath.

Having tamped down her queasiness, she turned and lay across the bed. It would be hard to keep the news of the baby from him for much longer. If she waited until he got around to confessing his love for her, as she wanted him to do, the child would be born and grown, with a family of his own. Her hopes were unfounded, but the fact he hadn't pursued a divorce gave her hope. Of course, he probably hadn't pursued it because he feared she might still be in danger, and his overblown sense of obligation to her father kept their marriage intact. But sometimes he looked at her...

She sat up on the bed, her wave of nausea gone, and decided to join her husband, father, and Grammie for breakfast. Though she couldn't stomach any food yet today, she looked forward to the cheerful fire in her father's dining room, and the leisurely time she spent with her family. Even though the relationship between Grammie and her father remained noticeably strained, she always found the conversation stimulating and their temperaments easy and infectious, even if not towards each other.

She entered the warmth of the big house. She'd grown fond of it, only second to Raine's smaller one she wished they shared. As she made her way to the breakfast room, she turned over how she would break the news to Raine. He'd be angry, but maybe he would give in and make love to her, seeing that no further damage could be done. She really must have lost her mind, for that to be her main concern.

She summoned a smile, along with her courage, as she entered the dining room. She bent down, placing a kiss affectionately on her father's cheek, and bid him a cheery good morning. Raine followed her with his eyes, but she couldn't face him yet. He would have that half-amused smile on his face that always made her feel as if she had milk on her upper lip or some such nonsense, so she ignored him.

Sitting at the table and placing a napkin in her lap, it dawned on her she was famished. Smiling at the realization, she ladled a heaping portion of the scrambled eggs from the serving dish onto hers and nabbed a richly buttered piece of toast, as well. She should have stuck to the toast, because as soon as she put a forkful of eggs in her mouth, her queasiness returned. Bowing her head and closing her eyes, she pulled her reserved strength to accomplish chewing and swallowing the too-soft eggs. Then she made the mistake of opening her eyes, which were directly focused on the plate of the runny yellow stuff in front of her. She slapped her hand over her mouth and ran from the room, retching into her hand.

Raine and Tom jumped up and ran after her. Tom yelled for Ruth, his housekeeper and cook, but she stood already attending Millie, who vomited into a pot Ruth held for her.

Raine fetched a pot of cool water and a rag while Tom stood by helplessly, watching his daughter empty her gut. When her spell subsided and the queasiness ebbed, Ruth took the puke-filled pot away, and Raine carried Millie to the sofa, laying her head on a soft pillow.

"Better now?"

She nodded feebly, afraid to look at him when she whispered words for his ears only. "Yes, it's just that I'm...it's only the..." She pulled the cool cloth away from her face. Seeing the concern and confusion on his face, she wondered how such an extremely intelligent man could be so obtuse. "Baby," she finished weakly with a sigh.

"Good God!" Raine exploded from the sofa as if his arse were on fire, and he began pacing. Her father stood nearby, and she wondered if he'd heard her whispered confession. If so, he hadn't reacted verbally.

****

Raine wondered, too, from the wide-eyed expression of shock on Tom's face. Was he frightened because his daughter had spent the last five minutes puking her guts up, or because he realized his trusted friend had seduced his daughter? Either way, he had some explaining to do.

"Tom," Raine began nervously. "In my stories about our trip, when I mentioned the part about our false wedding," he resumed his pacing, not at all liking the fact that he felt like a weasel in a trap of his own making. He'd surely bungled this-at everyone's expense. "Did I mentioned the fact that Millie and I, that Millie and I, that we really are married?"

Tom's face fell, his face an emotionless mask. "Uhhhh, no. I don't recall you mentioning that part."

Raine nodded absently. "Well," he winced, "we are. And," he continued, stopping only to run his hand through his hair, "Well, now...You see...It seems... Uh..."

"Out with it, boy," Thomas bellowed. "Is she going to have a baby or not?"

Raine looked up, stunned. "Yes," he exhaled. A ghost of a smile flashed across Tom's face.

"What's going on?" Margaret asked as she shuffled into the room.

Tom, in his reluctance to converse with Margaret, grunted, cleared his throat, and scratched his head, all in rapid succession. Finally, he turned on his heel and walked out of the room.

Raine plopped down on the sofa at Millie's feet and covered his eyes with his hand. "I'm sorry," he told her. "I've certainly botched this whole thing." He looked at her to gauge the emotions on her face.

Millie's green eyes locked with his. He tried to wordlessly convey the regret and contrition he felt, the guilt of their predicament weighing heavily on his shoulders. A flash of anger crossed her features, and the abruptness of it confused him. If he'd thought she was feeling sorry for herself, he was clearly mistaken. As he grasped for the words to assess and understand her unexpected wrath, she coiled her leg back and thrust it toward him, enthusiastically kicking him.

****

After several days, alone in the line cabin on the far end of the ranch, the realization of being a father settled in on Raine and had an effect he never could have imagined. The thing he feared most, having someone who would depend on him and look to him for protection, now seemed to be the only thing in his life worth living for. It became his driving force. Millie, with his baby in her, became something he wanted with an intensity that shook his soul, which is why he could no longer sit around and wait for Reynolds to make his next move. The time had come to ferret him out. Before he could go to Millie and declare his love for her, before he asked for her to deem him worthy of her, he must prove himself and his love for her.

Chapter Twenty-Three

It had been almost a month since Millie had surprised them all with the news of her forthcoming baby, and Millie reckoned it had been that long since she'd seen the sun. She'd not seen hide nor hair of her so-called husband either, for well over two weeks. He'd moved in with her, at her father's strenuous insistence, and then he'd disappeared after the tension became too much. Everything had happened too fast, she rationalized, and Raine had not had the chance to get used to the idea of being a father.

Millie wished she could stop thinking about him, curse his hide. The cold, snowy evening pressed against the cabin walls. She stoked the fire listlessly, then threw the poker in the corner, wanting to cry, but bored with even that. She'd holed herself up in her cabin, first hurting over Raine's departure, then fuming at him, and then hurting over him again.

A loneliness had descended upon her with Raine gone. Even though they hadn't been intimate recently, they still had been in each other's presence constantly, until now. A vast hole remained where he used to be, and she missed his company.

Her father suggested she sleep in the main house with Raine gone, but on that point Millie would not concede. In Kansas, she had reveled in her independence and the peace it afforded her, and she needed some of that now. She needed her privacy. To keep her spirits up, she lied to herself repeatedly, telling herself Raine had left for a good reason. But she really couldn't imagine what had taken him away, except for the fact that he now found himself with a pregnant wife, a wife he never wanted.

Her spirits may have been sagging, but physically she'd never felt better. Her nausea had magically disappeared, her health flourished, and her energy increased. She doubted that anyone's home had ever been as clean as hers. Sitting in her rocker, facing the stove, her feet propped on a small stool, she affectionately rubbed her belly beneath her robe. Her stomach barely mounded, but she loved the round curve where her baby rested. The light from the lantern cast a sleepy glow on the room, and the warmth of the fire relaxed her. She leaned her head back and drowsily listened to the crackling and popping of the fire. Contentedly dozing off and on, she resisted crawling into her lonely bed.

Several hours passed before Millie awoke with a stiff neck and decided to take refuge under the heavy blankets awaiting her. She reached into the woodpile, grabbing a stout log to carry the fire through the night. She snuggled her front up to the now blazing fire and stretched, soaking up the warmth with every inch of her lean body.

As she stared broodingly into the flames, a sudden draft wrapped sharply around her bare feet. The flames of the fire flickered against the onslaught of the unwelcome cold air. The click of the door as it closed made her heart pound in her chest, because she knew without looking who stood behind her. She turned. Raine stared at her, the flames of the fire reflected in his hungry eyes.

"Can I stay here tonight?" he asked.

She lifted her shoulders in a slight shrug without saying a word. Her voice would betray her turmoil.

He came up behind her, standing so close that she could feel the heat of his body, almost as warm as the fire in front of her.

"I know you think I ran out on you. I should have realized what my leaving meant." He paused, and she held her breath. "I've been thinking, though. Maybe we should try being man and wife for a while. What do you think?"

She wanted to ask him if he'd still want to try if there were no baby, but she wouldn't. She didn't care, at the moment, why he wanted to be with her. Instead, she turned and threw her arms around his neck and pressed herself against him, clinging to his hard body.

He kissed the dark, curling hair at her temple. She raised her eager lips to him, and he descended upon her offering, possessing her mouth. Raine scooped her up and took her to the bed, locking his lips once again to hers. Falling down upon it with her, he wrapped his arms around her as if to swallow her body with his.

"You missed me." He grinned unabashedly.

Millie pushed herself away. "You are the most arrogant man I've ever met."

Raine kissed her again, then stood to peel the wet clothes from his tired body. She watched him, intensely hungry for the sight of him. Discarding his clothes, he went to warm himself by the fire, and Millie watched him with awe.

"Where have you been?" she asked, hoping she

didn't sound too possessive, at the same time trembling from the magnificent sight of his backside.

"At the line cabin."

"Why?" she asked.

"I needed time to think. And I thought you could use the same. I know you're angry with me, and I don't blame you. I'm sorry about everything."

He turned to her then, and the look in his eye startled her from her musings. He didn't want to talk, and suddenly she had forgotten what they'd been talking about. He descended upon her painstakingly, pushing her back and lowering his long frame upon the length of her. His hand ran up her bare thigh, the texture and warmth of his calloused palm causing a tightness between her legs and in the pit of her stomach. He loosened her robe, and her arousal mounted, anticipating the feel of his hard body full against her skin. She was unprepared when his lips left hers and traveled downward. Lingering only for a moment at her breasts, his mouth then journeyed farther over the curve of her stomach.

He kissed her stomach north, south, east, and west, placing the last kiss on her navel. Surprising her further, his voice broke with emotion. "It's not near as big as I imagined."

She raised herself on her elbows, looking down at the top of his head while he kissed her there again. She could feel his hot breath tickling her belly. "It's only been two weeks since you've seen me."

"Much longer since I've seen you naked." He brought his face back up to hers, and the longing in his eyes bore a hole in her soul. "Too long."

She wrapped her arms around his neck and pulled him down to her. There were no questions that needed to be asked, nothing left unspoken needing to be expressed. He was there, touching her, kissing her, just as she'd dreamed of so many times since the last time they'd been together, and she would savor every last inch of him for as long as she could.

****

The next morning, a fully clothed Raine sat on his haunches next to the bed, staring at the sleeping form of his wife, and he tenderly brushed several curls away from her face. He would leave before the sun rose.

"Millie," he whispered. She groaned and reached out for him, and he placed himself in her arms. Neither he nor Margaret had told Millie about her relation to Parker Reynolds. But now he needed her to know. He needed her to understand why he had to leave. "We need to talk," he told her. Releasing her hold on him, she buried her head in the pillow and grunted a response.

"Parker Reynolds is your blood cousin."

Millie lifted her head and pushed her auburn curls out of her eyes. She gave him her full attention.

"He was Bridget's brother, not her lover, as I'd believed. Your mother had a brother, who left home at a young age. Your grandmother disowned him, and from what I've been able to find out about him, she was wise to do so. From what your grandmother has told me." His lips formed a grim line. "Insanity runs in her family."

Millie frowned back at him.

"Beauty has checked the adoption papers for me to verify the relationship. Apparently, Parker sought Bridget out several years ago. My guess would be to see if she had any money he could rob her of, and that is probably when he started courting you."

"Bridget tried repeatedly to talk me out of marrying

Parker," Millie shook her head. "She wouldn't have done that if she'd been involved in this. If he was her brother, then her loyalty to him blinded her." She looked at Raine with pain in her eyes.

"Chances are she tried to beat him to the money and didn't want him to have control of her share, since you were to oversee her trust. My guess is she realized she'd never see him again if he got his hands on it. She wasn't wrong there. Odds are, Parker killed Bridget."

Millie nodded. "Is Grammie still in danger? He wouldn't dare touch her now, would he?"

"She's safe here." Wrestling with the strong desire to crawl back in bed and hold her, he looked at her and whispered, knowing his next words would anger her. "I have to leave now."

"Where are you going?"

"Cheyenne. And if that doesn't pan out, Denver."

"That will take forever," she whined.

He smiled slightly. "I need to go. I need to find something that will prove Reynolds's guilt in your cousin's murder."

"Can't you let the law handle this?"

"Pete can't leave town."

"What about Beauty?"

"He's doing something else for me," he told her.

"Oh." She rolled away from him, pulling the covers up around her neck and avoiding his gaze. "Well, be careful."

Reluctantly, he stood to leave. Stopping at the door, he turned. "Goodbye, Millie."

She answered him, though her words were barely audible. "Goodbye, Raine." He stood in the doorway catching one last glimpse of her, then putting his hat securely on his head, he turned out into the bitter darkness just before dawn.

The trip wasn't as difficult as he'd expected. The weather had cooperated with mostly sunny skies. And once he'd ridden out of the mountains, the temperatures had stayed in the twenties, as far as he could tell. The furs he wore from head to toe made him immune from the constant wind beating the Wyoming plains. The weather stayed fair until his return trip, and even then, the snow held off until he neared home.

The record hall in Cheyenne had been a dead end, as he'd feared it would be. But in Denver he'd found what he'd been looking for. Reynolds had filed a new will for Margaret, naming himself as beneficiary along with Millie. Margaret's signature was on it, as well as some witness Reynolds had obviously bought. Comparing the signature on the new will to the old woman's signature he'd acquired from Margaret showed them to be alike, though in a contrived, rigid sort of way. Hopefully, the copy of Margaret's original will, which they'd sent for from Topeka, would be in Pete's office any day. Margaret would need to contest this new will, formally stating the signature had been forged, and that the document was a fake. Then Millie's inheritance would be protected from Reynolds. But what about Millie and her grandmother? Would they be safe?

Yes, the trip had been wearily accomplished, and it had been nearly fourteen weeks since he'd left. The snow had been falling heavily in the mountains, and travel back to the ranch would be slow. This time of year, even though it rained in town, the wet, early spring snow always fell heavily at the ranch. He'd hoped to be home before this happened, but he'd known the chances were slim.

Millie would be hurt and angry, bound to think the worst. She'd tell herself he avoided her, avoided his duties at the ranch, because of the baby, even though he'd tried to explain otherwise.

But in all honesty, he missed her. Perhaps Tom had been right when he'd accused Raine of being lonely. He hadn't realized to what extent until Millie came into his life. He felt alive being with her. And loneliness weighed on him when away from her, leaving an unsettled void. He couldn't explain it. He only needed her in his life. He could never have predicted wanting her as he did, but now it seemed like his lifeline. And so, the time he'd spent alone in his hotel room had seemed like a jail term.

Raine sat in the bar's corner, nursing the same drink he'd had for over an hour. All evidence indicated Reynolds would show his face in town any day. Beauty had been trailing him and returned to report Reynolds would be in the area soon. He would make his move. Raine had the feeling he would show up at the saloon first. He and Beauty had tracked Reynolds's movements for some time now, and there were several things he'd learned about the man. First, he had some pretty hefty debts, gambling being one of his more prevalent vices, his other vices being drinking and whores. In every town, without fail, he'd gone straight to the saloons and brothels before conducting any business.

Raine watched the saloon doors, scrutinizing every man who passed through the doors. He'd never laid eyes on Parker Reynolds, but he'd know him on sight.

After an hour of standing at the bar, Pete joined Raine at his table. "Maybe he's not coming." This game frustrated Raine. He couldn't wait here for Reynolds forever. Perhaps he should go back to the ranch and come back tomorrow night. He could spend this time making up with his wife, which, in all honesty, was all he really wanted to do.

Chapter Twenty-Four

When the rain decided to finally let up, the days became glorious, if not still just a little cold. With spring in full stride, there was much to do on the ranch, and Millie fell into doing what work she could still do easily and gladly. She'd continued riding, despite her growing state of pregnancy, rationalizing she'd always been more comfortable in the saddle than in any chair. She steered clear of unfamiliar terrain, new horses, or fancy riding.

In the lower hills behind the main house, she raised her skirts and awkwardly lowered herself under a towering pine. She often rode into the woods behind the ranch to sit and contemplate the turns her life had taken in the last year. Her belly was now a considerable portion of her body, as every breath reminded her. She thrilled at the life inside her, especially when the baby moved. She only wished Raine were here to enjoy it with her. As if he even cared.

Tracking down Parker and prosecuting him for Bridget's murder consumed him. She should be grateful. The image of Bridget lying in that bed, pale and lifeless with the single derringer shot in her chest, never wandered far from her mind. But she also lamented the loss of something she'd never had. At night, she tossed and turned with dreams of Raine. He'd been attentive before he'd left, and he'd been above and beyond what she could have ever hoped to find in a lover. But during his absence, she doubted their brief interludes.

She should have been content with work and with the growing baby he'd given her. But she missed the simple things other husbands and wives shared. Holding hands, idle conversation, even the arguing. Millie missed it all. She missed Raine and feared that no matter what passions they'd shared physically, they would never find their way to basic love, as she'd hoped.

His attempt to find evidence against Parker was noble and right, but damn him for so easily being able to walk away from her. He'd made no pretense about not wanting to marry her. Being a ridiculous dreamer, she'd convinced herself he'd developed feelings for her.

Closing her eyes, she attempted to let go of her turbulent emotions, but instead of relaxing, an uneasiness filled her. She couldn't shake the feeling of being watched. She looked around the wooded area, but nothing indicated another presence. Even so, she became instinctively ill at ease.

The respite she'd sought in the beauty of the mountains wouldn't be found today. Her uneasiness rapidly gave way to fear. Images of Bridget flashed through her mind. Feeling helpless under the weight of her stomach, she stood. Her already rising panic intensified with her thoughts of protecting the baby. She grabbed Outlaw's reins, chastising herself for disobeying her father's orders about going out alone, despite the derringer she'd brought for her protection.

When a snap on the ground behind her startled her, she swallowed the scream of terror rising in her throat, and reached down for her gun.

A man grabbed her wrist, staying her hand. The

familiar voice, close to her hear, greeted her with a deceptively smooth pleasantness. "Dear Millie. How are you? It's been a while."

She shuddered, but she straightened, facing him.

Parker took a step back and crossed his arms across his chest. "I've seen your husband in town," he told her, his voice smooth and insincerely charming. "He frequents that brothel fairly often, doesn't he? Has he tired of you already?" When Millie didn't respond, he continued. "Don't worry about it, though. I'll have to kill him, of course."

"Why is that?" she asked, with a calm she didn't feel. Inside she was frightened, but she refused to show it.

"He took what I wanted." He looked up at her from under a mop of wavy hair, flashing her a devious smile.

Sheer will allowed Millie to stand her ground.

"The money will be mine whether either of you lives or dies."

Jack barked and yipped, the sound not too far in the distance, and she looked over her shoulder.

"I know you're confused about where your loyalties lie, having to carry the man's child and all," Parker backed away from her. Openly sneering, he spat his next words at her. "But I don't intend to lose what's mine." With that he disappeared so suddenly, Millie could only stare at the thick stand of trees where he'd disappeared.

She turned and ambled down the hill as fast as she could, pulling Outlaw behind her. Absorbed in her shock at being face to face with Parker, Millie made her way back to the house, and then Raine was there, with his arms enclosing her safely in them. She mentally shook herself, uncertain she hadn't dreamed it all, that she wasn't dreaming of Raine now.

He turned her face to him.

"I'm all right." She removed herself from the comfort of his arms. "Parker was here. I went out for a ride, and he appeared." Relief washed through her bones at Raine's presence. Jack's strong tail beat against her leg, and she looked down at him with her best frown. "Where were you?" she scolded.

"He met me on the road about half a mile up, barking his fool head off." Raine released her and guided her to the step. She sat down obediently, and Jack climbed up and put his head on her knee asking forgiveness. Millie scratched him behind the ear.

At that moment, Tom walked out the front door. "What the hell was that dog barking at? Oh, hello, Son. Welcome home. You took your time."

Raine looked up, a concerned frown darkening his features. "Reynolds was here."

A range of emotions crossed Tom's face.

"Stay with Millie. I'm going to find him." Raine gave Tom a look intended to stay any argument.

Millie reached out as Raine turned to leave and grabbed his arm. "I know you realize this, but he's dangerous. He's not right in the head."

Raine nodded. "So I gather. I'll be back. Stay with your father until then." He bent to kiss the top of her head, then turned, mounted his nearby horse, and left.

Tom looked down at his daughter, concern deeply etched. "Millie darlin', are you all right?" he asked.

"I'm fine." She smiled reassuringly over her shoulder. Millie shuddered, remembering Parker's threats.

At her ashen expression, Tom lifted her to her feet,

leading her inside the house. "Let's get you inside. Are you hungry?"

Millie shook her head. "Is Grammie around?"

"She's in the study drinking my whiskey."

Millie's expression softened. "I appreciate you taking us in. I know she can be cantankerous sometimes."

"The truth is, and don't you dare tell her this, but I've enjoyed her company."

Millie stopped. She looked at her father with doubt. "I don't believe that, but you are sweet to try to put me at ease." She stood on tiptoes and kissed him on the cheek, causing him to blush.

He chuckled. "I'll never get used to that, but I'm willing to spend the rest of my life practicing." He looked at Millie with love and affection in his eyes. "Let's go find your grandmother."

Millie held back. "Do you think Raine will find him? Will he be all right?"

"Raine is the most capable man I know. You don't need to worry about him, love. He can take care of himself. And he's not going to let anything happen to you or the baby. I wish you trusted him, like I do."

"Hummph," Millie snorted.

"Let's find your wily old grandmother and see what she's up to. I'm sure you could use a distraction while we wait. And I want to make sure she doesn't drink my bar dry."

****

Several hours had passed when Raine returned. Millie dozed on the sofa as Raine explained to Tom and Margaret his failure in finding any trace of Parker. He let Millie doze a bit while he shared a whiskey with them.

"I am beyond frustrated with this," Margaret grumbled. "That man has pushed my patience beyond its limits."

"I know. Mine too. But he'll misstep." Raine suggested. "He was reckless to show up here. We know he's in the area now, and it won't take much to pin him down. Pete's on the lookout, as well as Dixie. He'll be spotted."

Millie groaned, breaking the hush of the conversation. She struggled to sit up, bleary-eyed and sleepy.

"I should get her to bed." Raine helped lift her off the sofa by the elbow. He looked at Tom. "We'll talk tomorrow—make a plan."

Tom nodded.

Millie leaned down and kissed her grandmother on the cheek, then her father.

Millie shuffled to the door with Raine at her side. She slipped on her coat and waited for Raine to do the same.

Raine reached around her for the door. "Let's go, beautiful," he whispered, his voice thick.

Overwhelming emotions welled up within her. "Beautiful, yourself," she bit out, as she elbowed him soundly in the ribs.

He grunted from the impact and put one arm around her waist and one hand on the offending elbow to prevent further assault.

"Let go of me," she protested. The nearness of him after his long absence, her encounter with Parker, and being so dreadfully round and large, all came together to cause a storm of emotions.

****

205

He whispered hoarsely. "Why should I, when all I've wanted to do is hold you?" He turned her around in his arms and immediately recognized her wrath.

Angry fire sparked in her eyes, so he attempted to pacify her. "I'm sorry I've been a less than dutiful husband, but Reynolds is not cooperating. The man has no sensitivity to the plight of newlyweds, I'm afraid."

She brought her heel down sharply on the top of his foot, bringing a cry of outrage and pain from him. He suppressed his own rising anger, knowing hers was warranted. Her fear fueled that anger, and his best course of action would be to distract her. He had a few ideas about how he wanted to do that.

Breaking his hold on her, she turned to walk away under her own steam, but he held her fast and stepped in front of her.

He brought his face closer to hers and asked, "Feeling neglected?"

Tears rose in Millie's throat, as they seemed to do over almost any little thing these days. "Right now, I'm feeling nothing but big and tired." She turned again to leave.

He stood planted, crossing his arms across his chest, contemplating her form. "Can you make love like that?"

Her mouth fell open.

He pulled her into his arms. "Do you know how hard it's been, being gone, when all I could think about was coming home and touching you again?"

She raised an eyebrow and looked down at the lump between them. "I can well imagine."

"God, that looks uncomfortable." His eyes drifted to the roundness of her stomach.

She turned her face away from his. "If you think I'd

give you the satisfaction of knowing you caused me any discomfort, you don't know me."

Raine exhaled audibly. Overcome with vulnerability almost alien to him, he faltered. "Millie," he searched her face. "Are you unhappy about the baby?"

She wrapped her arms around her stomach and looked down at it. "That's the only thing you've done right, as far as I'm concerned."

Relieved to realize hurt pride fueled her anger, and not something he couldn't fix over time, he pulled her back into his arms and she melted against him. He grazed her ear with his teeth. "Besides saving your life," he breathed. "Besides making love to you until you screamed."

Her face suffused with color. Breaking his embrace, she left through the front door. "I never screamed." She walked carefully down the front steps, ignoring him.

Raine let her get a few feet from him, perhaps for his own safety. "But you wanted to."

Millie picked up her pace to a near run. "Go to hell!"

Chapter Twenty-Five

Millie continued home with Jack on her heels and the secret hope that Raine would follow her. Damn, but that man could be irritating. Equally as galling, she couldn't stay mad at him. She loved him, backward and forward, inside and out. She turned, hoping to catch one last glimpse of him. Satisfaction bubbled and lightness buoyed her steps to see he followed her, head down, a ridiculous grin on his face.

"Would you like a hot bath?" he asked once they were inside.

"More than anything. There's hot water on the stove." She closed her eyes and leaned her head back. Raine nodded and prepared her a tub. He helped her undress, nudging her on at her attack of modesty, and lowered her into the bath. He then pinned her mass of hair up and lathered a rag to wash her back. Sitting spread legged on a stool behind her, he hesitated only a moment before rubbing her neck and shoulders with the soapy rag.

"I can do that myself," she protested meekly.

"I enjoy doing it," he answered. His tone held a note of warning to halt her protest. The absence from her made the task enjoyable, as well as extremely difficult. His breathing became ragged, and his heart labored. Her beautiful body, lush with the pregnancy of their child, thrilled him.

Millie took a deep breath. "He said he intended to kill you."

"Is that all?" He leaned forward. "Is that what had you so upset, that he threatened to kill me?"

His smug tone tweaked Millie's ire. "No, that's not all, but I think you should take it seriously."

"I am taking it seriously."

Millie relented, her voice trembling. "Parker's being here is no little thing. I didn't know what he'd do." One arm wrapped protectively around her belly.

Raine wrestled with several emotions. Rage. Fury. Fear. Possessiveness. Reaching over her shoulder, he cupped her chin in his hand and turned her head so he could place a comforting kiss on her velvet temple. He brushed a kiss on the corner of her mouth but sat back up to resume bathing her.

She let out a ragged breath. "How do you make me forgive you so easily?'

"What am I being forgiven for?"

"For abandoning me."

"I had to be gone. You know that. I now have evidence against him. What else?"

"Hanging out in brothels." Millie cursed herself for saying that. "I know I have no right to be angry. You never wanted to be married. Still…it hurts."

Discarding the rag, he firmly massaged her shoulders and neck. "I haven't been with anyone else." Relaxing against him, she could feel her tension drain through his fingertips. She rolled her head and let him work out the rest of her worries. She rested her head against his thigh. He took the soap in his hands, working a lather between them, and placed his hands above her breasts. As he rubbed her neck and shoulders with his soapy hands, she sighed. When his hands moved lower to cup her breasts, she arched, giving him full access. She gripped the sides of the tub, and his hands moved down around her hard, protruding belly.

Biting her bottom lip, she smiled and buried her face against his leg. "Ruins it, doesn't it?" she murmured against his thigh.

"Huh-uh," he grunted, the denial huskily uttered against the top of her head. "Not for me, sweetheart."

Millie grabbed the floating washrag, and slung it over her shoulder, slapping it against him. "You're insufferable."

"Maybe." He traced her jawline with the back of his knuckles. "But I haven't been married so long that I'd let a little thing like that stop me."

"You don't intend to make love to me." Her tone was incredulous.

He cupped her breast again as he kissed her ear. "I'm afraid I do."

Millie's humor faltered. "How?"

Grinning, Raine bit her earlobe, knowing she waited for an answer. He whispered his intentions in her ear. She sat up straight.

"Oh!" A flush stained her cheeks, and a throaty laugh escaped her. She considered his answer for a moment, and seeing the implications and the promise of it, she once again relaxed against him. With eyes seductively lowered and head supine against his leg, she reached her dripping arm up and pulled his head down to her. Offering him her neck, she worked her fingers in his hair as he kissed her there. She responded with a smile. "Yes, I suppose that will work."

****

Millie woke the next morning, content to lie in her warm bed and savor the memories of the previous night. The warmth of Raine lying next to her, his powerful arm draped over her, his legs entangled in hers, lingered in his absence.

Rolling over leisurely, she reached out to run her hand along the pillow where his scent still lingered. Her eyes flew open as her fingers touched something, and she smiled at the bouquet of wildflowers. She sat up as swiftly as her bulking frame would allow, but she could detect no other sign of him.

Hugging the small bunch of flowers to her chest, she smiled at the tender gesture, thrilled also, at the memories of their night together. She dressed eagerly, verifying her appearance no less than three times before deciding she looked fit enough.

She found Raine and her father sitting quietly, both men looking up when she appeared in the doorway. Tom stood to greet her, and she went to him, giving him a smile and a kiss on his cheek. Raine's watching eyes were warm.

She sat beside her husband. Hesitantly, he took her hand in his and moved his face close to hers. She smiled at him, and he responded by kissing her tenderly on the bridge of her nose. She sighed, closing her eyes and smiling.

"Good morning," he told her, his voice hoarse with subdued emotion.

Raine looked up to see Tom staring intently into the fireplace. The sound of an approaching wagon caught the attention of everyone in the room. Raine cut a sharp look at Tom and then moved to look out the window.

A well-dressed woman stepped down from the

wagon, short in stature, but striking even from such a distance. Her pale blond hair shimmered in the sunlight, and her small, but big-busted frame made Millie feel awkward and rotund.

"Who is she?" she asked.

Raine frowned. "Maybe she knows something." He pushed himself away from the windowsill and walked outside.

Millie turned to her father.

He frowned, his discomfort obvious.

"Is that Dixie? The one that runs the brothel?"

Tom's frown deepened. As Grammie joined them at the windowsill, the three watched as Raine approached Dixie, and she wrapped her arm around him, hugging him close. She whispered something in his ear, or perhaps even kissed him.

Millie covered her mouth with her hand as she watched the scene. Seeing that no one paid heed to her, she walked out the back door and escaped to her cabin. "I haven't been with anyone else," she mocked. He'd lied about that, obviously. They were bound against his wishes, and the weight of that burdened her. And Raine, too noble to walk away, would honor his commitment. But she wouldn't settle for an unhappy marriage of convenience. She'd find a way out of this mess. And as soon as they'd put Parker behind bars, she would take the baby and Grammie, and would go home to Kansas.

****

When Dixie drove up in front of the house, an alarm went off in Raine's head. He didn't miss Millie's hurt expression, but he dismissed it. He could appease her misplaced jealousy later. He went outside to see why she'd come.

Dixie pulled him close. "Oh, Raine. I'm so glad you are okay." She hugged him tightly. "He bragged that he'd killed you." She choked on her words.

"Is he at your place?"

"Yes, he's still there, still sleeping."' She pulled back. "He was incredibly drunk, and it'll probably take a while for him to sober up."

"I'll ride into town with you, and you can tell me what happened. Wait for me."

Raine turned toward the stable, where he passed Jake. "I'm going into town."

Jake grunted his consent. Taking his cigarette from his lips, he asked, "That dude fella caught yet?"

Raine looked around. "Not yet." He wiped a drop of sweat from his forehead with his thumb. "I've been doing things by the law up until now, but I'm through waiting. We all know what the bastard did."

Jake took a long drag off his cigarette, and pinching it between his thumb and finger, removed it from his lips. He blew the smoke out the side of his mouth and squinted at Raine through the cloud.

Raine clasped Jake on the shoulder as he walked by him and muttered, "Keep an eye out for me here, okay?"

Jake nodded and walked on.

Raine went straight to the great room and looked directly at Tom. "I'm going after him. I'm done waiting. I'll kill him if I have to, but he's not getting away again."

Tom nodded his head. "Be careful."

"I will. Now, Millie…" Raine looked around the room for his wife, but he didn't see her. He put his hands on his hips and scowled angrily. "Where the hell is Millie?" He looked between Margaret and Tom, but neither had an answer.

Tom shook his head guiltily. "She disappeared when we weren't looking."'

"Damn it!" Raine bellowed, swiping his hat off his head, and slapping it against his leg. "Can't she keep that damned temper of hers cool for five minutes?" He looked again between Margaret and Tom, as if they would know, but their blank stares only made him angrier.

Margaret spoke up. "I'll see to Millie, son. You go after him. And you be careful. My granddaughter needs you, even if she is too stubborn to say it."

Raine nodded and put his hat back on his head, tugging it down to secure it. He turned to the back of the house, heading for their cabin where she would undoubtedly be sulking. Millie stood by the stove with her arms crossed angrily. "She's just a friend," he bellowed. "Stay here." He pointed at her, commanding her to stay put. "Don't go anywhere. I'll be back." He closed the door, only to open it again. "She's just a friend!" He slammed the door behind his last words and rode off to town.

Chapter Twenty-Six

Raine sought out Pete immediately and relayed the latest incident with Parker Reynolds, his threats to Millie, and Dixie's visit to the ranch. From what Dixie had divulged, he'd had a considerable amount to drink, so they hoped to find him still in his bed. However, he'd disappeared by the time they arrived, slipping through Raine's fingers once again. Raine's patience had long run out. He didn't think Reynolds would be bold enough to go back to the ranch so soon, so he decided he and Pete should wait for him to show himself in the bar.

Hopefully, Reynolds was equally eager for a confrontation. Reynolds had to get him out of the way, before he could possibly pursue Margaret's fortune, and Raine was willing to bet he would come for him. So here he stood, in Dixie's bar, waiting for Reynolds to show himself and hopefully have it out.

A man Raine didn't recognize walked through the doors, and even though many strangers wandered through town, he would have remembered this one. The man looked out of place, but then he probably would have looked awkward anywhere, with his patchy clothes and deformed appearance. The unfamiliar man walked straight for the bar, leering toothlessly at one woman perched there. Dixie had always told her girls they didn't have to accommodate any man they couldn't abide, and Raine had a feeling this man would walk away unsatisfied tonight. Undeniably ugly, he attracted Raine's attention despite, or perhaps, because of it.

"Know him?" Pete asked, following the direction of Raine's unwavering gaze.

Raine shook his head. He couldn't understand why the man drew his attention. He stood at the bar, looking around uneasily, obviously searching for someone. Finally, Raine's gaze locked with his, and recognition was evident before the man looked away nervously.

Pete picked up his drink casually and talked into it. "He knows you."

Raine stared at the back of the stranger's balding and unusually round head, and then locked eyes with him in the mirror behind the bar.

Pete stood and adjusted his gun belt. "Partner, if you don't mind, I'm going to get out of the way," he mumbled, looking out over the room. "Do me a favor, though. Make it clean."

Raine only nodded, never taking his eyes off the wiry man at the bar, though that man's gaze fluttered anxiously around the room to avoid Raine's threatening attention.

Pete went to stand at the opposite end of the bar from the man and looked casually around the room. Raine watched the pumpkin-headed man finger his gun shakily, before placing his hand back up on the bar. A wry smile played across Raine's lips as the man checked to make sure the gun still rested at his side. Reynolds had sent the man here to do his dirty work, no doubt. The path lay open from him to the stranger, and Raine's quelling looks kept it that way. The man didn't look smart enough not to try to kill him, and he looked just clumsy enough for his bullet to find the wrong target, so

Raine wanted to make sure he killed the man cleanly, as soon as he turned to fire. How he wished Reynolds stood in his sights, challenging him. But that would come. Raine waited, anticipating the man drawing on him, when he noticed the man locking eyes with a second man for a brief second.

Raine's gaze darted back to the ugly stranger, and he watched as the man's bulbous nose twitched in a nervous gesture. It gave him away. The man turned hastily, sliding his gun out of his holster, and aiming for Raine. Raine's bullet lodged in his chest, causing the man to fire in the air before dropping his pistol. Blood soaked his already grimy shirt, and he dropped to the floor.

All movement stopped, and Raine's eyes immediately went to the second man. He could see his hesitation as the man's arm jerked uncertainly, obviously trying to decide if drawing on Raine was such a wise choice. Gunfire rang out as Raine shot three glasses off the bar in front of the man in warning. The man stilled his motion, then turned to look at Raine, raising his arms in the air. But his eyes revealed his intention a split second before he reached for his gun, ignoring Raine's warning. He didn't clear his holster before the killing bullet struck him.

Raine holstered his own pistol and walked to the dead men. The talking and laughter resumed as if nothing had happened, as if everyone had just been given a great show.

"What happened to my nice, quiet little town?" Pete grumbled at Raine's side.

"He's not here," Raine stated blandly.

Pete shook his head as he reached down and grabbed

the arms of the first body. "No, I'd say not. Come on, son. Help me get these bastards out of here. This one smells so bad, the flies will carry him off if we don't."

Raine bent to help Pete with the body, and the smell reminded him of the man Millie had described, the one who'd held her in the cabin where Bridget had been found. He remembered Millie's revulsion and looked down at the man in his grasp. If it had been this man, he couldn't help but shudder at the narrow escape she'd made.

After dropping the bodies outside for the undertaker's care, Raine mounted up and started home. Parker could have found Millie and Margaret already, and that awareness created a twinge of anxiety. Tom and Jake were there to protect them. Raine doubted Reynolds could get within a hundred feet of either of them. He spurred his horse forward as doubt and anxiety gripped him.

****

Millie wrestled with a tumult of emotions. As an adult now, she should start acting like one, including not running from the unpleasant aspects of life. For her own sanity, she needed to pursue the divorce. It had been a possibility haunting her since the first time she realized she loved Raine. At least she would know by his acceptance or refusal of it what his feelings on the matter were. If he didn't want the divorce, he would tell her so. If he did, at least she'd be bowing out gracefully and holding up her end of their agreement, instead of throwing a fit of hysterics as she wanted to do.

She couldn't help worrying with Raine still in town. Grammie had explained the reason for Dixie's visit, and Raine willingly walked into jeopardy to protect her. She shouldn't have acted so childishly, but she had so many doubts. Waddling uncomfortably to her father's house, groaning with the difficulty of the extra weight she carried, she noticed a movement in the barn. It should have been empty at this time of day. Hopefully Raine had come home, and she could put her worries to rest.

When Millie arrived at the stables, she found no sign of anyone. Raine must be around here somewhere. She turned for the tack room to look there, but when she did, Parker stood casually against a stall post.

"I wasn't sure which one of you I would find. I'm satisfied with you." His tone taunted, but his eyes hinted at the madness lurking behind them. He shook his head and clucked his tongue at her. "All of this would have been much easier if you'd cooperated in the beginning. It hurt my pride when you preferred him to me. What could he possibly have offered you? Surely not status? It must have been wealth."

"Something you could never understand." Millie balled her hands into fists, trying to calm the seething fury which engulfed her. If she had to do battle with the enemy, she would need her head clear for rational thinking. "Anyone who could kill their own flesh and blood hasn't even the slightest concept of love."

Arching an eyebrow, he seemed genuinely surprised. "You love him? Ah, I hadn't counted on that." Parker frowned and pushed himself away from the wall with his shoulder. "Bridget wasn't exactly a saint, now, was she? But I never intended for her to be killed. She should have learned you can't treat people like trash, even if they are." He shrugged. "She went too far with my colleague. You remember him? I imagine you would have suffered the same fate had you stuck around. He was not happy with you."

Parker looked up at Millie with a smile, his hand resting on the back of his neck. "But you bested him, didn't you? I say, Millie. You've been full of surprises."

Millie shuddered at the fear Bridget must have suffered facing death at the hands of that horrid man. "You had her killed. It's the same thing as if you'd done it with your own hands."

"Do you think so? Well, maybe you should know that our dear Bridget tried to convince me to kill your...our grandmother. I didn't think it necessary until she made me see the advantage of it. Until then, our marriage would have satisfied me because the old woman would never recognize me as her heir. She disinherited my father, after all. But Bridget wanted everything. Actually, she made me see the logic and benefits of killing you both. Then you had to go and get married. The list of people in my way became too long. That's why we must end this now."

"Surely you don't think you are going to come out of this unscathed? Everyone is looking for you. They'll follow your trail back here. They'll be here any minute, I'd say."

"Good. I look forward to finally getting rid of that half-breed husband of yours." He began to pace in a short, furious stride.

Millie turned and ran down the short corridor to the back of the stables. When she spied Jake's body sprawled on the ground outside, fear halted her. He lay there, bloody and beaten. Was he dead? By the looks of his battered body, and the amount of blood on the shovel which had obviously been used to beat him, he wasn't far from it. She detected a small movement from him, and she breathed a sigh of relief.

"Millie." Parker's voice was menacingly hard. She turned. His pistol pointed straight at her. "I'm warning you."

Millie's only concern was protecting her unborn baby. She grabbed at the first inspiration to enter her mind, anything to distract him. "Parker, you can have the money, you know. It's not as important to me as it seems to be to you. You leave now, and I'll arrange for you to have it."

"It's a little too late for that now, don't you think?"

"Then what do you want?"

"Revenge. I want revenge for being cheated out of my rightful inheritance. I want revenge for you having enjoyed all these years, what should have been my father's and then mine. And I want revenge on your husband for taking what I deserved."

"If you think for one minute I've ever been privileged to Grammie's money, then you're wrong. She's given me nothing. If you think Raine has received any money from marrying me, then you're wrong again."

Parker shook his head. His hollow laugh rang in Millie's ears, like a ghost roaming an empty hallway. "Your husband is another matter. He will have to be out of the way. And our grandmother, well…"

A movement at the far end of the stables behind Parker caught her eye. She tried not to make any indications that would give away what she'd seen.

She prayed silently for help, when Grammie appeared out of nowhere with a rifle in her hand. She raised it to take aim and fired. The shot hit a lit lantern, which fell. Taking advantage of Parker's surprise, Millie grabbed a rake leaning against a stall. She knocked the gun from his hand before catching him around the leg, upsetting his balance. He fell to the floor with a thud, and both women ran. Millie stopped only long enough to grab another lit lantern from the wall and throw it in the dry hay on the floor behind her. It ignited immediately, creating a wall of fire between her and Parker, and she turned again and ran for the house. Millie's feet carried her heavy load with amazing speed as she grabbed Grammie's hand and pulled her shuffling along behind her.

****

Raine became increasingly alarmed as one of the ranch hands rode hell-bent towards him, calling his name.

Sliding to a halt in front of Raine, he shouted, "There's a fire. At the ranch. I don't know how bad it is, but we could see the smoke from the north pasture. The boys went to see what they could do. I came to recruit help."

"Go find Pete. Tell him what's going on, then find Doc Wallace. We may need him." Raine kicked his horse and took off toward the ranch, saying one of the few prayers he'd recited in his life. He pleaded for Millie to be at home, safely watching his life's work burn down, because none of that mattered. He only wanted her.

Chapter Twenty-Seven

Raine arrived at the ranch just as the stables collapsed, sending sparks spiraling to the black abyss above. The form of a man lay sprawled on the ground. Spurring his horse toward the injured man, Raine jumped down and gathered Jake in his arms.

"Hey partner, you okay?" Raine asked softly. Blood ran from Jake's ear and from a large gash at the temple. The blood and bruising made his face almost unrecognizable. His left leg and stomach were also bleeding. Raine couldn't see the extent or cause of the blood, but his injuries were serious. He persisted, hoping Jake was coherent enough to answer. "Can you tell me where Reynolds is?"

The light faded in and out of Jake's green eyes and Raine's heart sank. "Hang in there, partner," he told the semiconscious Jake. "Help is on the way."

Raine moved Jake away from the blazing barn to safety. He walked out into the night and looked back over the horizon, hoping help would arrive soon.

Suddenly, a scream tore through the night.

"Raine!" Millie's terrorized outcry pierced Raine's heart. Not wasting a breath, he started for the back of the house, where Millie had called for him. As he slipped into the shadows surrounding the house, he removed his white shirt, making him less obvious in the waning light. His instincts surfaced. Movement inside the house alerted him. He backed up against it, listening. Suddenly, the back door flew open, and Parker roughly shoved Millie out of it. She stumbled on her skirts, but Parker grabbed her and pulled her back against him by a handful of her loose hair, then roughly dragged her down the porch steps. The steel gun in Parker's hand flashed blue as it moved to Millie's temple, and Raine became blind to all else. Millie was alive, and Reynolds would be dead in minutes, by his hand, and that thought alone calmed him.

He stepped out of the shadows, looking at Millie first, unconcerned with Parker or his gun. Raine understood why Parker might think he held all the cards. He had Millie. Raine was unarmed. And when Parker took the gun away from Millie's head and pointed it at Raine, he must have assumed nothing could stop it all from ending easily. Parker seemed to want to savor the moment.

Raine moved then, carefully walking toward where Reynolds held Millie. Only when Raine stood a few feet away and yet still approached, did Parker's countenance falter, and his eyes show uncertainty at Raine's boldness.

Parker pulled the hammer back on his pistol, but still Raine moved forward.

****

Millie watched it all with an appearance of detachment. Under the weight of her exhaustion, she didn't have the strength to fight anymore. She had to trust Raine to do her fighting for her. As Parker cocked the gun, and still Raine came toward them, adrenaline washed through her, and she stiffened. Her eyes fixed on Parker's hand, and she watched, and she waited.

Why didn't Raine stop? Why was he still coming

toward them, toward a certain death? She pinned her gaze on the hand that held the means to end Raine's life in its palm, memorizing the creases engraved in the knuckles. Then she perceived a slight twitch of the tendons in his wrist. He was going to shoot. She screamed and knocked Parker's arm at the precise moment that he pulled the trigger, sending the bullet into the side of the house and evicting a chunk of wood. Parker cursed loudly and pushed her away from him.

He turned once again to take aim and shoot, but too late. Raine had begun to charge him, an unsettling roar tearing from his throat. Parker scrambled for control of the pistol, but Raine was upon him before he could take aim.

Raine hit him full force, and as both men landed with a thud on the hard ground, the gun flew from Parker's hand, landing in the dust several feet away from the scuffling men.

Clutching her belly, Millie scrambled to get to her feet from where she had fallen. Grammie grabbed her arm to help her up, and she checked Millie over to verify her well-being. Millie's attention focused completely on her husband now, but she welcomed Grammie's comforting arm around her waist.

The sound of galloping hooves had brought Tom in from the north pasture. He stood watching the two men, his hand on the pistol at his side. "I should have known Parker let the stock out. Millie, are you all right, darlin'?"

She nodded. "Can't you do something? Help him!"

"Raine would have my head if I interrupted this fight. He's been itching for it for too long. He can hold his own. Reynolds isn't going anywhere, now, except to jail. Let your husband have his pound of flesh."

Raine and Parker wrestled in the wide expanse of dirt between the house and the barn, light from the low-burning stable fire illuminating their forms in the darkness. Raine overpowered Parker and began pounding him with his fists, each blow finding its mark with frightening precision and power. Parker didn't have a chance against Raine's fury. His body jerked and rolled with each pain-wrenching blow he received.

But with each whimpering cry Parker made, Raine lost his passion for killing his enemy. It brought him no satisfaction to beat his weaker opponent. Raine slowed his assault on his victim but pinned him in place. Raine watched his quarry huddle beneath him with his arms protectively over his head, anticipating the next blow.

"If you want to live a few seconds longer, Reynolds, you'd better fight for it," he threatened, as he loomed over his huddled form.

He released Parker and watched as he scrambled out from under him, shrinking away in fear for his life. Damn the coward! Leave him for the law, after all.

Wrapped up in the scene before her, Grammie moved away from Millie and walked in a semicircle around the group and back again, like a cat circling its next kill.

"Hell fire," she brooded from her position behind Raine. "I'm too old for this horse poop." Squinting for her aim and drawing an unsteady bead on Parker, she raised her rifle and fired a shot. Everyone froze, except for Raine.

He fell forward helplessly, clutching his shoulder while confusion clouded his brain. Millie shouted his name. His injury wasn't fatal despite its impact, and raising himself to his knees, Raine watched as Parker scrambled in the dust for his pistol. Finding it suddenly in his grasp, Parker turned and took careful aim.

Suddenly the sound of cannons resounded in the air as three rifles fired at once, and Parker's lifeless body fell in the dirt.

****

Raine looked uncertainly at his shoulder again, at the blood oozing there. He welcomed Millie's warmth pressed against him as she dropped to his side. He turned to look at her, finding solace in her soft, moss-green eyes, relieved beyond words that she was unharmed and her ordeal over. Everyone stood in a circle around them, Pete and Tom still holding their rifles on Parker's still form. The old woman shuffled toward them, her rifle resting on her stooped shoulder, concern resting on her wrinkled brow.

Raine looked at Millie. "Your grandmother shot me," he barked.

"I did not!" Margaret's voice held censure, a considerable frown marking her brow.

"You did too! And you did it on purpose."

Millie lifted her skirt and tore off a piece of her undergarment to wipe away the blood. She dabbed at his shoulder, absorbing the blood, and revealing the clean hole from Grammie's bullet. "The bullet went through." Relief washed through her. "It doesn't look too bad."

"Maybe not," he admitted reluctantly, "but if she hadn't been so drunk, she probably would have killed me."

"I ain't drunk, you dunderhead." Scowling, Grammie crossed her arms across her chest.

"Since when?" he growled.

The others had closed in, concerned about Raine's

injury. While all eyes turned on Raine and Grammie glaring angrily at each other, Millie groaned and clutched her protruding middle. All eyes riveted toward her.

She recovered, attempting to act as though nothing had happened, but as she looked around, stunned faces gaped at her. Exhausted already from her long struggle with Parker, she gladly conceded her dilemma, though her pale face continued to wear an expression of scorn.

"Well," She looked at Raine, trying to lift herself up, "if you don't think you're going to bleed to death…"

Raine grabbed her arm, concern in every line of his face. "Are you all right?"

"Yes," Millie assured him, "but if you're going to live, I'm going to go in and have this baby."

Chapter Twenty-Eight

"Damn, this is good whiskey."

"Good, I'm glad you like it. I admit I didn't want to read that first letter you sent me." Raine happened to be walking by Tom's office on his way to see Millie, and he couldn't help but overhear Tom and Margaret. Since Margaret first set foot on the ranch, they'd been ducking down hallways, hiding behind buildings, trying expressly to avoid each other, but grunting and snapping when an accidental confrontation did occur. Happy they were finally working it out between them, he started back up the stairs to see his wife. However, Margaret's next sentence and triumphant tone halted him.

"But everything has worked out as we planned, after all. I'm glad they did it all on their own, and we didn't have to persuade them. I knew they would. I knew it from the moment I met Raine. Let's drink to Millie and Raine."

Raine still had a hard time believing they had duped him so easily. He'd found out about their plans when he'd read Margaret's will, that they desired an arranged marriage between the two of them. He couldn't believe either Tom or Margaret would have forced the marriage, but the wording of the will made it evident they would have given the two of them a hell of a time getting out of it.

"I liked your Raine immediately," she continued.

"He was everything you said he would be, though I hadn't counted on that stubborn streak. But I suspected, just as you did, that they were perfect for each other. And I certainly hadn't counted on all this other unpleasant business. I figured just telling her I sold the ranch would be enough to get her out of there. I didn't know I'd end up coming, or that we would have to be terrorized all the way up here."

Raine couldn't help himself. He stood there, paused on the steps, and listened, looking around guiltily on occasion.

"I certainly hadn't counted on you coming," Tom narrowed his eyes. "Not that I mind. But it was one thing to write letters over the years. Seeing you face to face was something I wasn't prepared for. I had a lot of anger stored up for a lot of years, Margaret."

"Can you ever forgive me, Tom? Can you forgive an old woman who's lived with years of regret for what I did to you?" Margaret's voice cracked with emotion. "I can only hope I served you well in the way I raised her, and that you can enjoy a long future with her and many grand young'uns."

"Margaret, I couldn't have hoped for her to turn out any better than she did at your hand. I've learned not to mourn for the past. My life has been full, thanks to Raine. I hopefully have many years left in me to…"

Raine turned from the door and started up toward Millie's room. Drifting up the stairs, Margaret's incensed voice came to him.

"This is my whiskey! How the hell did you get my whiskey?"

Raine smiled. He could just imagine Tom's gloating expression. Astonished at those two, he shook his head, and his smile turned sentimental. It didn't matter now how he and Millie had come together. If it hadn't been right for them, he wouldn't feel the way he did about her. He looked at the papers in his hand, and his smile soured. He loved Millie to distraction. Now she wanted a divorce, but he would not let her go without giving their marriage a chance at a new start.

****

Millie rested comfortably, reclined on the bed against some pillows, nursing Maggie, their new daughter. Raine entered the room where she'd been sleeping the last two nights since the baby had been born, and his expression communicated his reason for being there. He'd received the papers. She flinched when he threw the envelope on the bed at her feet.

"We're not getting a divorce."

Didn't he know she didn't want one? "Okay, Raine."

"Is that all you have to say? No screaming fit? No show of hysterics that I'm making you stay married to me?"

"No, Raine." She shook her head. "I didn't want a divorce."

"Then what the hell are these for? You filed for it. I assumed it was what you wanted."

Millie unlatched the baby from her breast, laying her on the bed and covering herself, but not before Raine stared with open admiration at her bare breast. She blushed at the intimacy of having him witness her nursing their daughter.

Raine turned his attention to the baby and seemed to forget about Millie for a moment. He picked Maggie up before Millie could, wincing at the pain in his healing shoulder. He turned his back and sat on the edge of the bed. Tears welled up in Millie's eyes at the deep, soft words of love that Raine cooed to his daughter. Millie had hoped that she, and not only the baby, kept him from wanting a divorce. But his love for his daughter was evident. She'd seen no evidence of his feelings for her.

She stared at his broad back, up to the slight wave of his black hair at the nape of his neck. How she wanted to reach out and touch him, but fear of rejection stopped her. How did their relationship stand? She still didn't know, and not knowing crushed her. Just then, the baby let out an enormous belch, causing them both to laugh. Raine turned to look at Millie. Unshed tears welled in her eyes. He handed the baby back to her and stood awkwardly.

He scowled and asked, "You don't want a divorce?"

She shook her head, trying to hold back the sobs that seemed to want to burst forth. She bowed her head, her loose hair veiling her face.

"Then why are you crying?"

"I…can't…help it," she wailed, the sobs uncontrollable now.

Raine's expression of horror displayed his complete loss. He sat down again, this time next to her, and he pulled her across his lap, wrapping his arms around her and the baby. Millie cried into his chest for several minutes before she could subdue her tears. Raine pulled back and offered her his sleeve, which made them both laugh.

She handed him the baby, crawled off his lap, and grabbed a handkerchief from her nightstand. She turned to face him and sat back against the pillows again. Wiping her eyes and honking loudly into the handkerchief, she tried to regain some semblance of composure. She wiped back and forth across her nose and looked back up at Raine.

When she met his eyes, the laughter there revealed his amusement.

"It's good to see you smile." She offered tentative words. "I'd forgotten how pretty it was."

"Pretty?" He straightened, his expression wounded.

"Handsome." She grinned and bit her lower lip. Their eyes locked. A force drew them together. He was going to kiss her, and she wanted him to, but suddenly he stiffened.

She looked away uncomfortably and changed the direction of their conversation. "I'm sorry I burnt down your stable."

"Don't be. Those stables were here before we were. They were poorly designed and too small. I look forward to building new ones."

"You're just saying that to spare my feelings."

Raine shrugged and smiled. "True." And then, locking eyes with her, he added solemnly, "But do you honestly think, for one second, that I would have traded those stables for your life?" The baby cried out, and he handed her to Millie. "Hey, speaking of gorgeous, she sure is, isn't she? It's not just me, is it? She's really pretty."

"Yes, she is," Millie nodded in agreement, turning her attention to the instantly sleeping baby in her arms, smiling lovingly. She gently laid her on the bed beside her and smoothed the covers surrounding her tiny, huddled form. Straightening the covers across her own lap, she busied herself to avoid looking at Raine. She wanted to have him hold her and laugh and talk with her like they did for a brief time. She wanted to tell him she loved him, and hear those words from him, but too much uncertainty existed between them. Perhaps, in time, they could be like they were.

"How's Jake?"

"Mending," Raine answered. Their eyes met and Raine cleared his throat. "Do you want me to build you a fire?"

She smiled and nodded. The nights were always much cooler, and she would need the warmth of the stove.

He reached for the papers. "Mind if I use these to start it?"

Millie shook her head. His gesture didn't express an "I love you", but it seemed like a start, a new beginning for them both.

Chapter Twenty-Nine

The snow had come late this year. The few flurries in November had not amounted to much. Everyone, including Millie, enjoyed seeing the snow falling in time for Christmas. Decorations of sage, candles, and big red ribbons adorned Tom's house. A great round pine stood by the window adorned with ornaments of brass, lace, paper, and popped corn. The eggnog tasted rich and potent, and it flowed freely. The fire in the hearth could have been a mere reflection of the warm and inviting room it burned in, but it popped and sparked with a life of its own.

"Old woman, you'd better let up on that stuff," Raine scolded.

"Son, I'm almost seventy years old. You get to be my age, and you can tell me what to do."

Raine received such enjoyment out of antagonizing the old woman. But he feigned a scowl. "How do you think it looks, an old woman like you, drunk all the time?"

"I didn't give a damn what people thought when I was younger, and I care even less now."

Millie entered the den with her fat baby, having just finished her feeding, and laid her in Raine's arms. With black hair and searching, cerulean eyes, Maggie McConnell, though only three months old, was unquestionably the spitting image of her father. Raine smiled warmly and carried his daughter over by the tree to play on the floor.

Millie surveyed the scene, her family and friends, all in their Christmas cheer. She thrilled at everyone being together again. She'd received an early Christmas present. Raine had sent Beauty all the way to Kansas to bring her best friend, Lydia, as well as Lydia's mother, Miriam, to Wyoming to spend several months with them. What a surprise it had been when Lydia had introduced her fiancé, none other than Beauty himself—dirty, smelly, hairy, John Reichman. But this time he'd been clean-shaven and, well, unbelievably pretty. No other word could describe him. She still couldn't believe that under all that hair and dirt had been a beautiful, intelligent man. She was truly happy for her friends.

The spirit of the season had touched her greatly with the arrival of Lydia, John, and Miriam, but today she didn't feel entirely cheery. She still didn't know where she stood with Raine. If only he had ever said it, even just once, Millie would have no doubt that he loved her. They laughed and talked, often as if the best of friends.

But every time things became serious, every time the physical tension seemed too much to bear, Raine changed, becoming polite and distant. They hadn't made love since before Maggie was born. Would this be the way of things? A loveless marriage in name only? Millie didn't know if she could stand being so close to him and unable to touch him, physically or emotionally.

Millie approached her father, wrapping her arms around his waist, and burying her face in his shoulder.

"I've never seen him so happy."

She turned and walked out without a word. Tom followed her into his study.

"Millie darlin', what's wrong?"

"I wish he hadn't thrown away those divorce papers," she told him.

"Woman, what are you talking about? You'd be hard-pressed to get a divorce out of him now."

"Because of Maggie."

"Because of you. Don't you know how much he loves you?"

Millie walked to the window and looked out back to the cabin she once shared with Raine. "He has never said as much."

"Does he need to?"

"If he acted like he loved me, then no, I wouldn't need to hear it." She looked back at her father, pain twisting her face. "But he doesn't act as if he loves me. He's given me no reason to believe he does. He's only staying married to me because of Maggie. I know he can't give her up, but I can't live like this. And I won't give her up, either. It's an intolerable situation."

"Young love," Tom mused. "How fragile it can be. Have you told him?"

Millie's expression remained impassive, but her emotions were in turmoil. She continued to look out the window at the falling snow, her hands in fists at her sides. She bowed her head and pressed it against the cold glass. "No," she conceded grudgingly.

Tom's hearty laugh reverberated through the halls. "Women!"

Millie shrieked in outrage. "You two. 'Women'," she mimicked. "Is that your excuse for everything?"

Tom sobered. "We just don't understand you." Tom crossed his arms. "Has it ever occurred to you, daughter, that perhaps he is just as uncertain of your feelings for him? You did file for divorce, remember?"

"He made it clear from the beginning that he didn't want to be married, that he wanted a divorce as soon as possible."

"Millie, every man thinks he wants to remain single. The notion of getting married scares the hell out of most of us. But obviously, things changed. If he had no feelings for you, he could have easily resisted your charms. There'd be no Maggie, and we wouldn't be having a need for this discussion."

"Father, I am not so naïve that I think a man has to have 'feelings' for a woman for that to happen." Millie blushed. She didn't like the turn of this conversation. She hadn't known her father so awfully long that she felt comfortable talking with him about such an intimate thing.

Tom displayed no embarrassment, but a display of temper began to show at the depth of his daughter's stubbornness.

"Then you don't know the man at all. He's not a weak man, subject to whim, and if you hope to get anything out of him, I suggest you swallow some pride and give a little of what you expect."

Tom was unaware that his voice had risen until Raine filled the doorway and purposefully cleared his throat. "Unless you want everyone in on whatever it is you're arguing about, I suggest you temper it a little." Millie cast an angry glare at her husband. She squared her posture indignantly and took her leave, careful not to touch Raine as she passed him.

****

Holding his daughter against his shoulder, Raine watched Millie walk by with her nose in the air. He tried desperately to suppress the urge to turn her over his knee and settle things finally, suppressing that urge only because he didn't know if that would work any better than doing what he really wanted to do: throw her down and make love to her. God knows he'd tried being patient, but that had gotten him nowhere. His patience, along with his self-restraint, nearly threatened to make him demented. "I'm in it again, I see. Any idea what I did this time?"

Tom turned his back on Raine, trying his best not to laugh. When he regained control of his humor, he turned to Raine with the most serious look he could summon. "It's like this. As near as I can figure, the girl still has doubts that you care for her."

"She wants me to care for her?"

Tom rolled his eyes. "Yes."

Raine rubbed the back of his neck. "And she doesn't know I care for her?"

"'Fraid not."

Raine looked at his daughter and then back at Tom, the absurdity of the conversation wearing on him. "And she wants me to tell her how I feel?"

"Yep," Tom admitted again.

"All right…" Raine laughed softly. He turned with a new resolve to find his wife. He entered the den full of family and friends. He handed the baby to Miriam, who immediately cuddled Maggie's small form to her.

Raine left Maggie in the care of Miriam, Lydia, and Margaret, before walking over to Millie. He pulled her up from where she sat in front of the fire and led her over by the window for some privacy. He took her in his arms and turned her face to his, then kissed her, savoring the feel of the length of her against him. Pulling back to look

Deb Ransburg

at her, he searched her green eyes, detecting obvious doubt. He leaned down and kissed her again, so sweetly and so tenderly this time that the tears welled up in her closed eyes. Her pulse quickened under his fingers, and her breath left her in a heated rush. She could no longer have any doubts. The devotion in his kiss expressed it all.

He pulled back again, only a little this time, and looked down into her upturned face. "Millie, I love you," he whispered, as he wiped the tear from her cheek with his thumb.

She opened her eyes, searching his face. He hoped she would never again have reason to doubt.

"I love you too, Raine."

This time louder so that everyone in the room turned to look at them, he said, "I love you."

"Okay," she whispered, embarrassed by the attention they had drawn. "I believe you. Sshhh."

Raine threw back his head and laughed loudly, squeezing her against his chest. "Mildred McConnell," he shouted at the ceiling, "I love you."

Millie pushed herself away from him, scolding him with her best glare, brilliantly disguising her absolute joy. Then she turned, no longer able to contain her smile. She didn't miss a step as she winked at the three women around the Christmas tree playing with her precious daughter and exited the room.

As everyone watched her leave, Tom and Raine looked at each other. Raine rolled his eyes and shrugged his shoulders, completely at a loss. He decided it was a good time to join Beauty in the eggnog's partaking and moved to pour himself a generous serving.

Miriam watched the two men and shook her head

with disgust. Handing the baby to Margaret, she gracefully stood and smoothed her skirts. Approaching them, she tugged Tom aside and whispered in his ear. Tom looked at Miriam, his embarrassment undisguised as he contemplated her message. She nodded encouragingly and pushed him forward. Tom hesitantly walked over to Raine and Beauty, and after a moment of standing there under their regard, with a sheepish look on his face, he leaned over and whispered in Raine's ear.

Raine's scowling features helplessly yielded to the grin that consumed them. He turned and watched his wife walking down the path through the snow to their cabin. As if she sensed him watching her, she stopped and turned. Placing her hands on her hips, she cocked her head. Snow landed in her hair and on her eyelashes as she stared at the window where her husband stood concealed by the frosty pane. Her mouth spread into a seductive grin, the only invitation Raine needed. He ran out of the house, slamming the door, and down the path to carry her home.

Beauty and Lydia looked at each other knowingly. Miriam walked back and took the baby, kissing her lovingly again in the crook of her neck. No one witnessed Grammie and Tom exchange glances. Everyone missed the extra twinkle in their eyes, and so they were blissfully oblivious as Tom gave Grammie a triumphant wink and a victorious smile.

A word about the author...

Deb Ransburg enjoys her rich and busy life in Soldotna, Alaska. She loves spending time with her grown children and grandchildren, as well as exploring the beautiful Alaskan wilderness. She is a teacher, a writer, and an artist. Her daily struggles include keeping her nose out of books so she can write, cleaning up the mess she makes while painting or making pottery, and preventing the weeds from overtaking her garden.

https://www.instagram.com/debransy/
https://twitter.com/paiganwrite
https://www.debransburg.com/